PROUDLY THEY DIE

Center Point
Large Print

Also by Lewis B. Patten and available from Center Point Large Print:

White Warrior
Ambush at Soda Creek
Lynching at Broken Butte
The Angry Town of Pawnee Bluffs
Ride a Tall Horse
Red Runs the River
The Guilty Guns
Massacre at White River
Rifles of Revenge

PROUDLY THEY DIE

LEWIS B. PATTEN

CENTER POINT LARGE PRINT
THORNDIKE, MAINE

This Center Point Large Print edition
is published in the year 2025 by arrangement with
Golden West Inc.

Copyright © 1964 by Lewis B. Patten.

All rights reserved.

The text of this Large Print edition is unabridged.
In other aspects, this book may vary
from the original edition.
Printed in the United States of America
on permanent paper sourced using
environmentally responsible foresting methods.
Set in 16-point Times New Roman type.

ISBN: 979-8-89164-398-7

The Library of Congress has cataloged this record
under Library of Congress Control Number: 2024944862

PROUDLY THEY DIE

CHAPTER ONE

He halted his horse atop a long rise where the land was sprinkled with scrub timber and stared ahead at the crowded plain.

His face was lean and dark and troubled. His cheekbones were high and prominent, this being a legacy from his mother, who was full-blooded Sioux.

But his eyes were grey, and they narrowed as he saw how scrawny and thin were the steers in that distant pole corral. Hunger can bring only trouble and the bellies of the encamped Indians out there were too empty to be filled for long by this handful of scrawny steers.

Impatiently, Will Jordanais touched his horse's sides with his heels. The animal moved ahead.

Nineteen, was Will, this year of 1890. Nineteen and torn unmercifully between a heritage as strong as the Sioux and Cheyenne blood running in his veins and a way of life, the white way, in which he had been raised.

Directly ahead of him lay the building of Pine Ridge Indian Agency, covering, perhaps, five acres of ground. Behind them, some distance away, lay a long, low bluff. Immediately around the Agency was only open, rolling prairie. There was no stockade.

On Will's right, a couple of miles from the Agency buildings, was a pole corral containing the steers which were to be issued to-day. There appeared to be about a hundred, these to feed the more than two thousand Sioux who had assembled for the twice-monthly beef issue.

Beyond the corral lay the Indian villages, stretching away for miles, each separate, each forming a rough circle. Closer, the Indians were grouped, with their women, their children, their dogs, their horses.

Around the corral itself they were ten deep. And before the gate, their chiefs and headmen clustered, waiting.

Even at this distance, Will could detect anger in the way their heads were held, in the way they gestured and talked among themselves. A rider suddenly left the corral and pounded hard toward the buildings of the Indian Agency. Will had halved the distance between himself and the corral before he saw the man returning at the head of a detachment of Indian Police. The murmur of angry voices began to grow.

His own tension increasing, Will searched through the crowd until his eyes found the two he sought, Goose Face and Red Bird. Patiently and slowly, he eased his horse toward them.

Angry, smouldering eyes turned to look at him. Most of the Indians knew him, yet gone was the acceptance he had known among them once. Of late they trusted no one who was not full-blooded Sioux. There were even those among their own from whom they had withdrawn their trust. And a feeling of tenseness was in the air, compounded of anger and resentment, a feeling that promised violence.

Knowing how his father felt, Will knew he ought to turn and ride away. Yet he did not, but continued instead until he reached his friends.

They looked up at him, but did not speak. Will glanced again toward the corral, toward the group of whites immediately before the gate, now surrounded protectively by Indian police.

Always before the beef issue had been an exciting, laughing, pleasant thing . . . a mock revival of the old-time buffalo hunt. It was not like that to-day. Uncertainty and nervous fear showed in the faces of the two Agency employees who were in charge.

But the four ranchers who had supplied the cattle were plainly contemptuous. They had lived with the threat of Sioux violence too many years to believe it was imminent now. Besides, they were well aware that Indians never begin a fight with winter coming on. They wait for spring, when the grass is good and their ponies fat.

Will stared at the four and at the two Agency employees. Both outrage and anger were in his eyes. He knew the government paid for fat, prime beef. He also knew that there had to be dishonesty someplace or beef like this could not have been substituted.

Goose Face and Red Bird and a few young men of their band mounted and began to push towards the corral gate. Will followed.

One of the ranchers said loudly: "Let's get on with this. I can't stay here all day. I got other work to do."

Goose Face, now less than ten feet from the group, shouted, "No!" He turned his head and uttered a stream of angry Sioux. It was followed by a roar of approval from the crowd.

Goose Face and his young men advanced threateningly toward the whites. Reaching them, they crowded them deliberately against the gate.

Will stared down at the faces of the whites. He realised that this was rapidly getting out of hand. A member of the Indian Police brought his rifle up. The sound of the hammer cocking was loud and clear.

Will acted instinctively. His heels dug deep into his horse's sides and the animal plunged ahead. His shoulder struck the Indian policeman and pinned him solidly against the gate. Will reached down and snatched the rifle from his hands.

An Agency man yelled, "Stop it! Stop it, all of you!"

Will dropped the rifle to the ground. The Agency man stared up at him with hostility in his eyes.

The Indians behind Will apparently could not see what was going on. They crowded closer, until Will couldn't have moved if he'd wanted to.

Something had to happen. Someone had to calm the intolerable tension or further and more disastrous violence was inevitable. The Agency man shouted in the Dakota tongue, "All right. You'll get better beef next time. But this is all we got to-day! Now move back!"

A rancher bawled, "By God, I'll clear the bastards away from here!" He snatched his revolver out. Raising it, he pointed it at Goose Face's chest.

Will was nearly ten feet away from him. Pressed in from behind as he was, he couldn't move. And he wasn't armed.

Helplessly he watched. Then, so close that it deafened him, he heard a rifle shot. Smoke billowed over and around the group of whites. The rancher sagged back against the gate, but he didn't fall. He stood there, pinned upright by the press of bodies on all sides of him.

Blood spread from a spot on the front of his shirt. His mouth grew slack and his eyes grew dull.

It was done and the bullet could not be recalled. Something heavy and cold seemed to be filling Will's chest.

His father had told him that violence was inevitable. He had also warned that the Sioux had no chance to win. First violence would signal final throes of their dying race.

There was silence, briefly, more frightening than the noise had been. It was broken by an enraged voice, speaking the language of the Sioux. And from behind Will came a Sioux chief, mercilessly forcing his plunging horse through the crowd.

Will recognised him. It was Big Foot, who had lung fever and was known to be near death.

He reached the gate and whirled his rearing horse. He shouted angrily at the crowd. Reluctantly, sullenly, they pulled back.

Big Foot was shaken by a fit of coughing. His face grew dark, then pale. Sweating and almost grey, he controlled his coughing by the sheer force of his will. Speechless, he glared at Goose Face, at Red Bird, and at Will.

With his fierce old eyes he held them, until his voice returned. Then he reined his horse close to the young Sioux brave who had fired the shot. He took the man's rifle away from him. He turned his head and spoke halting English to the two Agency employees. "He no got gun. Take. Throw in calaboose. Try for killing. But better set him free. He shoot to save Goose Face's life."

Relief showed in the faces of the frightened and shaken whites. One of the Indian police mounted and rode to the young Sioux brave. He took the reins of his horse and led him through the crowd.

Two others lifted the dead rancher to a horse. One led the horse while the other steadied the limp body lying across the saddle.

Big Foot turned his head and addressed the crowd in their own tongue. "Now we will get on with this. There will be no trouble. The name of each village headman will be called in turn and when it is, a single steer will be released. It will be as it has always been in the past."

He glanced at Will. Surprisingly there was no distrust in his eyes, but rather a grudging approval. Will realised that Big Foot had seen what had happened earlier, when Will crowded the Indian policeman against the gate and took his gun from him.

The Indians backed away from the corral gate, opening a lane through which the steers could run. Will released a long sigh of relief. More violence had been avoided, for now at least. The business of butchering the steers would temporarily calm the Sioux, and for several days they would eat.

But when hunger came again . . . His face worried, Will stared at his friends, at Goose Face and Red Bird. He found himself thinking of Red Bird's sister, Teal Duck, whose Sioux name was Siya-Ka.

Red Bird shouted, "Come, Good Eagle, join us and help us down our steer!"

Will nodded, his face still troubled. Good Eagle

was the Sioux name his friends had given him because his English name came with difficulty to their tongues. Reining his horse around, he followed Red Bird and Goose Face to the end of the line now forming near the gate.

Tension was still present in the crowd, but now it was tension of a different kind. The Agency man called out the first name in a voice that trembled with relief.

The corral gate swung open and a single, wild-eyed steer bolted from the enclosure. He thundered along the lane that had been left open for him.

Instantly a dozen horses carrying shrieking braves raced in pursuit. Three of these men carried ropes, with the loops held wide by willow hoops. Several of the others carried rifles. Those remaining carried bows and arrows.

Those with the ropes rode in first. One after another they tried to drop their loops over the galloping steer's head, but he was too agile and wild. All of them missed.

Next, the braves with bows and arrows rode in. The first missed. The second put his arrow into the running steer's neck.

The steer's head dropped. His horn caught in the ground and he catapulted end-over-end and afterward lay kicking on his side.

From the waiting, silent crowd a roar of approval, and even though it was approval, the sound was like the uneasy murmur of thunder below a distant horizon.

Out of the crowd came the women and children of that particular band. They streamed across the prairie, some riding, some walking, some leading horses from which the poles of a travois dragged.

The women clustered around the downed steer like magpies, chattering excitedly. One cut the steer's throat to kill it, and the others began to cut it up. The children squealed, hopping excitedly on first one foot and then the other as they waited for raw titbits.

Will sat his fidgeting horse, watching, frowning lightly with his thoughts.

His first memories had been of a white man's town, of houses and stores, of a church bell pealing on Sunday morning. His first school had been a school in town, though by the time he attended it he knew he was different and he was familiar with taunts and with children's cruelty.

But he went doggedly every day, fighting when he must with an intensity and fierceness that discouraged further cruelty. He learned to write English, and he learned arithmetic.

When he was ten, his father and mother moved to the Dakotas. Here, for the first time, Will mingled with the Sioux, who often located their villages nearby.

It had been like coming home. They accepted him, and he wandered through their villages and played with other children his own age—played the games that Indian children play—games that were imitations of a grown man's tasks. He already knew the language, which he had learned before he learned English from his mother. And the Sioux had become his friends.

His father understood, but did not approve. Yet in spite of his disapproval, he never forbade Will the freedom of the Sioux villages. He had shown his son both ways of life. He knew Will must make the choice.

Will's thoughts were interrupted by the release of a second steer. He watched as a second group of mounted warriors took up the pursuit. And watching, something almost like pain briefly touched his eyes. This was a pitiful substitute for the buffalo hunt. It only emphasized the absence of the great herds of buffalo, the absence of freedom and independence that had been so much a part of the old life. The Sioux were prisoners now, clinging forlornly to the past.

Then the thought and the pain were gone, for another steer bolted from the corral with Goose Face, Red Bird, and the others in pursuit.

Will raced behind them, caught up as always with the excitement of it. He watched Red Bird as he veered in and shot the animal in the neck.

The steer, a bony, small animal with black and white spots and a broken horn, dropped.

The braves of Goose Face's band pulled their plunging horses to a halt.

For several moments, excitement lingered in their faces. The women and children of the band came running toward them in a ragged group.

Then, as though all at once they realised what a poor substitute this was for the old-time buffalo hunt, their faces turned blank and impassive and something almost like shame showed briefly in their eyes.

Will glanced around. Everywhere was the hubbub and confusion of butchering. Every few hundred yards there was a group, kneeling and working beside the carcass of a steer. Amongst these, at regular intervals, came another running steer, pursued by half a score of warriors, yelling, firing arrows and sometimes guns.

Will thought fleetingly that it was a wonder no one was killed. And then he saw, among those running toward the downed steer belonging to Goose Face's band, a girl he recognised instantly.

No one else ran like Siya-Ka, he thought. Like a young deer, or like a bird swooping along just above the waving grass.

She was part of his early memories, for he had known her since he was ten. And yet, something new and very sweet was between them now.

He saw the way her eyes were downcast. He saw the flush that crept up into her throat and face.

And he realised his decision had been made long ago. Whatever the fate of the Sioux, he would be part of it. He could not . . . he would not change.

CHAPTER TWO

He watched her steadily, watched each small movement she made. He remembered her as a girl of eight, remembered each stage of her development. He remembered once when she had pitched into a fight like a small wildcat to help him out, and he smiled faintly at the memory.

She was a beautiful girl, by the standards of either Indian or white. Her face had not the round fullness common in so many Indian women but was, instead, delicately and finely shaped.

Slight she was, and formed as a woman should be formed. The top of her head reached only to the point of Will's shoulder, but she was strong and did her share of the work. Occasionally she would peek at Will shyly out of the corner of her eyes.

She was dressed in fringed and beaded deerskins, old, worn ones, for butchering is not a task for which one wears her best.

The children of the band chattered like magpies, their eyes shining with excitement. The women skinned the carcass, leaving the hide spread out for it to be upon.

All the members of Goose Face's band grouped themselves around the steer. Liver, heart, and kidneys disappeared into their hungry mouths.

At last all were satisfied and the remainder of the carcass was carefully wrapped with the hide and loaded upon a travois. Not much, Will thought, to last the thirty members of the band for two weeks' time.

As he rode past the corral on the way to the village of Goose Face's band, he saw a rider arrive from the Agency buildings at a hard run. The man's eyes were frightened and his face was white. Will caught the words, "Four thousand hostiles from Rosebud. They'll be here . . ."

Others also caught the words and the rumour spread like a grass fire through the village of the Pine Ridge Sioux.

Will doubted if the rumour was true. But he knew it would be true if the course things were taking didn't change. Hungry Indians, afraid and desperate . . . whites who cheated and sneered at the Indians' dignity . . . a government too far away to know what was going on. The combination would have consequences that could only be violent.

A sinking feeling touched him. His father was right. The Sioux could not possibly win. Will knew, if their chiefs did not, what appalling strength the whites could muster if given time.

But no one seemed interested in stopping the course of events. The Sioux were too angry to care. Their beef issue had been cut far below that which had been promised them. They were being cheated out of much of what was left. Desperate, they listened now to the words of the self-styled Messiah, Quoitze-Ow, and they danced his Ghost Dance because they didn't know what else to do.

Not that the Ghost Dance could help. Will remembered his father's bitter words regarding it. "They're grabbin' straws, Will. They're desperate enough to do anything. That dance ain't goin' to help. It's fake. They just dance until they're all wore out and because they have dreams they think they see the face of God. Only they don't. They just dream it because it's what they want to dream. Naturally, their God says all the words they want him to say."

Will had to admit that he was right. Yet he also knew that he would not destroy the beliefs of his friends even if he could. The Ghost Dance was the only answer to their helplessness that they had found.

He stopped at the tepee of Goose Face. The headman was squatted before it. He looked up at Will with an impassive face, but with welcome in his eyes.

Will swung from his horse. He squatted beside the chief. "Do you believe the rumour that the Rosebud Indians are hostile and that they are coming here?"

Goose Face was silent for a while. At last he said, "There will be no fighting now. Others do not agree with me and are moving their villages. But I believe what I have said."

Will didn't know what to say. He did not agree, either. He felt that fighting would come, and soon.

He was young enough to feel a certain excitement at the prospect. Yet he could not forget his father's words.

He rose and started to mount his horse. Goose Face said, "I am going to the camp of Tatanka-yo-tanka on Grand River to-day. You may go if you wish."

Will had heard of the great Sioux medicine man, but he had never seen him. He wanted to ask why Goose Face was going to see Sitting Bull, but he did not. He nodded eagerly. "I would like to go."

"Good." Goose Face rose abruptly. "Go to the lodge of Red Bird. Tell him I wish him to accompany us." His eyes twinkled suddenly, "And you may tell Siya-Ka good-bye."

Will mounted and rode toward Red Bird's lodge. He dismounted and stepped inside. As he repeated to Red Bird what Goose Face had said, he watched Siya-Ka, busy at the fire in the centre of the tepee. Once she glanced up and flushed.

Red Bird said, "I will get my horse." He was plainly excited, as though he sensed that this visit to Sitting Bull was more than an idle journey. Red Bird had guessed, as Will had, that Goose

Face was trying to decide what he should do in the threatened trouble with the whites. His visit to Sitting Bull would decide the issue.

When Red Bird went out, Will remained. His words, in the Dakota tongue, sounded more formal than they would have in English. "You have changed. You are a woman now, and a very beautiful one."

He stared at her with sudden hunger. He wanted her, yet in his feelings toward her there was a tenderness he had not experienced in his relations with the half-dozen other women he had so briefly known.

She was a woman, and knew his need. For a moment her eyes met his bravely in spite of the fright that had suddenly appeared in them.

Almost harshly he said, "I am going to Grand River with Red Bird and with Goose Face to see Sitting Bull. When I get back I will bring gifts and horses to Red Bird."

Her voice was faint and small. "Siya-Ka will wait."

Will stepped out of the tepee into the cold sunlight feeling as though he owned the world. Then he thought of his father and the exhilaration faded. A moment ago he had committed himself irrevocably. His father would accept the decision but he would not be pleased.

Will mounted his horse and was about to ride away when he heard the voice of Siya-Ka behind him. "The journey to the camp of Sitting Bull is long," she said. "You will need food."

He turned his head and saw her standing before the opening to the tepee. In her hand she held a bag made from the outer skin of a buffalo's stomach. It was filled, he knew, with wasna, an Indian hash made by mixing finely ground meat, grease produced from the boiling of bones, and dried and powdered chokecherries. The whites called it pemmican.

Will took the bag she handed up and tied it to his saddle. "Thank you," he said.

He whirled his horse so sharply that the animal reared. Then he pounded away. But before he passed from sight among the clustered tepees, he looked around.

She stood watching him, unmoving, her hand raised to shield her eyes from the sun. She looked exactly as she would look if she were his squaw and he was riding away to fight. He felt a tingle run along his spine.

Will cleared the villages and rode out upon the open prairie. In the distance he could see Goose Face and Red Bird, riding fast. He kicked his horse's sides and hurried after them.

But for the incident at the corral, he realised, they would probably not have allowed him to go along in spite of the fact that he had known them both for years.

Catching up, he saw that the faces of both

were grim and he knew they had been talking.

He wanted to tell them that resistance to the whites was both useless and foolish. He wanted to tell them how many thousands of soldiers the whites could bring against them. But he remained silent.

Goose Face seemed to sense his thoughts. He said, "I know what you are thinking, Good Eagle. You are thinking of the land of the white men to the east. You are thinking that they can bring a hundred soldiers to fight each Sioux warrior. And I know that it is true. I have been through their lands and I know."

He was silent and frowning for a moment before he went on. "But I am a Sioux. I must do what the Sioux do. Some of them want war, others want peace. I must decide for those of my band whether it is better to die like a man or to live like a dog, snapping up the scraps they throw to us."

"Maybe that could be changed. If the government in Washington knew what was going on . . ."

Goose Face shook his head. "They know. They cannot help but know. Did not the government cheat during the counting of the Indians so that they would not have to give us meat for our children?"

Will knew he was referring to the census of 1881, bitterly criticised by all the Sioux because the census takers counted only adults and not children. The result had been that no beef issue was made for the children they had at the time of the census, or for those born later.

Goose Face went on resentfully: "They took our game and gave us nothing in return. They promised us, in the treaty we signed with General Cook, that each Sioux warrior would receive six hundred and forty acres of his own, to be his forever as the white man's land is his. But when General Cook died, his promises were broken. Nor would the white men send us tools so that we could make our living from the land. Even their promise to send us cattle has been broken. They have reduced the amount by two million pounds a year and we get only the cattle that the white men do not want."

Will nodded. Everything Goose Face said was true. He said, "Maybe it is only that the white men here are dishonest. If you told the government in Washington . . ."

"We have. Many times. Not five days past I put my name on a paper our chiefs sent to Washington. But we know that nothing will be done because nothing has been done in the past. It is a bitter choice, but the Sioux must either starve or go to war."

"What did the paper say?"

"It told the Great Father that when we gave up the Black Hills he promised that each Sioux should get three pounds of meat a day. He also promised that we would get other food like the white soldiers did. It said that we had received neither the other food nor the three pounds of meat. It said that if he did not want to give us what he had promised, then at least to send us a soldier for an agent so that the cattle we did get would be fat and strong."

He stared at Will. "You are of mixed blood, as your father is. You speak the tongue of the whites. But you have grown up among us and have been like a brother to us. You know I speak the truth when I say I do not want war. Nor does any other chief among the Sioux want war for they know they cannot win. But answer this, Good Eagle. Is it not better for a Sioux warrior to die fighting than to die of starvation in his lodge? In the days before the beef issue I watch the children of my village and I hear them cry for food. I see their thin bodies and know they cannot grow up to be strong and brave unless they have more to eat."

"Why do you want to see Sitting Bull?"

"Because he is wise and because he knows much of Quoitze-Ow, the Messiah. He has talked to those who have talked to that great one. At Sitting Bull's camp I can join the Ghost Dance. Perhaps I will see the Messiah for myself. Perhaps he will tell me what I must do."

Will could not help remembering his father's words, "Grasping at straws . . ." And it was true. Faced with two choices, equally impossible to accept, the Sioux needed someone to tell them which of the two they must choose.

The situation was made to order for the faker, Quoitze-Ow. But Will said nothing. It would do no good. Goose Face didn't believe in the self-styled Messiah any more than Will did. He was just forcing himself to believe because he didn't know what else to do.

They rode hard all the rest of the day, across endless empty plain, across ridges of pine-covered hills, across frozen creeks. That night they stayed with a small band of Brules in their camp beside one of the narrow, frozen creeks. Will was glad for the warmth of the tepees around him. He had brought no blanket and the night was cold.

They rode again at daylight, after having eaten some warmed-over dog stew given them by the Brules. At noon they ate of the pemmican Will carried in the stomach bag.

His thoughts dwelt on Siya-Ka as often as they dwelt on the problems facing the Sioux. He thought of the many velvet nights when they would lie together in each other's arms. He thought of the way her soft, warm mouth would feel against his own, of the way her hands would feel upon his face. He thought, too, of the strong sons that she would bear.

His body grew hot with his thoughts. He knew there had never been another choice for him.

His father might not approve, but he would not try to change his mind. Instead he would help Will gather the finest horses on the ranch for his gift to Red Bird, even though Will's choice saddened him.

Will and his father had talked many times about the problems confronting the once-proud Sioux. His father had often said, "They've just got to learn to live like the whites. They're finished unless they do. There's been too much change. The buffalo are gone. So they've got to learn other things—raise cattle and farm."

"The government won't let them do that."

"No." He remembered the way his father had looked as he shook his head. Sad, as though deep within himself he regretted the passing of the Indian ways, as though in his heart he loved the way of the Indian more than that of the white.

Will did not find it strange. His grandfather, though a white, had lived among the Indians and had taken an Indian wife. Only after his death had Will's father gone to live among the whites. And he too had chosen an Indian wife.

Will's mind continued to wander. He puzzled over the strangeness of contrast between the two races. The whites, outnumbering the Sioux overwhelmingly, still felt it necessary to boast of their victories over the Sioux. Yet the Sioux took no pride in their victories over the whites. They considered the killing of Yellow Hair at Little

Big Horn a simple act of self-defence and hardly one of which they could be proud. They had never considered it an honour to kill a white man since they believed the white men were weaker than they.

The Crows and Chippewas, however, their traditional enemies and their equals in battle, were quite another matter. They were proud of their victories over these.

All the rest of that day they rode, conserving the strength of their horses as much as possible. Again that night they stayed at an Indian village.

Will thought it quite possible that soldiers would be at Sitting Bull's camp. They considered him the leader of the impending revolt. They had ordered the Sioux to stop the Ghost Dance, and had threatened force.

But when the trio rode into Sitting Bull's camp the next morning there were no soldiers. There were only the Ghost Dancers, working themselves into exhaustion as determinedly as they could.

The three paused for a moment to watch the dance. Then Goose Face reined his horse toward a tepee upon which was painted the likeness of a buffalo bull sitting on his haunches.

They entered, careful not to pass between Sitting Bull and the fire in the centre of the lodge.

Silently they took seats upon the floor, facing the fire.

Sitting Bull's squaw brought him a pipe, which he lighted from the coals of the fire. He pointed the stem at the heavens, at the four points of the compass, and at the earth. He smoked briefly and then passed the pipe to Goose Face. Goose Face smoked, then passed the pipe to Will.

Will glanced aside at the great Sioux medicine man. He was not a big man, but he had the wisest, most penetrating eyes that Will had ever seen. He wore his long hair in two braids, one at each side of his head. His mouth was wide, thin, his nose long and straight. His was a strong face, one of the strongest Will had ever seen.

Goose Face said, "I have come to consult with Tatanka-yo-tanka. There are many rumours of war and I do not know what to do. If I fight, those in my village will die. If I do not fight, they will starve. Perhaps I should dance the Ghost Dance here at your camp. Perhaps I shall see Wakan Tanka, as others have, and he will tell me what to do."

Sitting Bull nodded thoughtfully. "There is a man in camp who has been to Nevada and seen Quoitze-Ow. Would you like to talk to him?"

Goose Face said that he would. Sitting Bull immediately dispatched his squaw to bring the man to him.

She returned shortly, bringing a tall, thin Indian

of perhaps sixty. He sat down and smoked with them. After a while, Sitting Bull spoke. "This is Goose Face and Good Eagle, who is part white, and Red Bird. They have come to hear of the Messiah."

"They are wise."

"Tell them the words of the Messiah as they were spoken to you."

The tall Indian hesitated several moments, as though assembling his words. At last he said, "I will tell you his exact words. Then there will be no chance for you to misunderstand.

"He told me, 'I am the man who made everything you see around you. I am not lying to you. I made this earth and everything on it. I have been to Heaven and seen your dead friends and have seen my own father and mother. My father told me the earth was getting old and worn out, and the people getting bad, and that I was to return and renew everything as it used to be and make it better. All your dead will be brought back to life. New earth will fall from the heavens and cover the old. It will cover the white men, but it will not cover the Indians so long as they keep dancing. But you must not fight the white men for that is bad. You must all be good and live as your customs have taught you to live. Then, when you are sick, I shall send someone to heal your sickness, and you will live forever.' "

The old man was silent.

Silence lay heavily within the tepee of Sitting Bull. In spite of his disbelief, Will felt a chill run along his spine. Almost angrily he shook his head. The Messiah wasn't stupid anyway. He had promised the Sioux everything a man can want, including everlasting life.

But he remained silent, for he knew that to scoff now would be extremely dangerous.

Besides, he didn't want to scoff. He didn't want to destroy the hope that had been born in Goose Face's eyes.

Goose Face turned to Sitting Bull as the tall man got up and silently left the lodge. "What do you think? What must the Sioux do?"

"Do?" Sitting Bull replied thoughtfully. "I do not know. I search my mind for the answer, but I always think only this. What treaty that the whites have kept has the Indian broken? Not one. What treaty that the whites made have they kept? Not one. When I was a boy the Sioux owned the world. The sun rose and set in their lands. They sent ten thousand horsemen into battle. Where are the warriors to-day? Who slew them? Where are our lands? Who owns them? Is it wicked because our skin is red, because we are Sioux, because we would die for our people and our country?"

Goose Face said, "I will dance. I have heard your words."

Sitting Bull replied, "So long as we dance, we

need not fight the white men. But if they make us stop dancing, then we must fight." He spoke sharply to his squaw and she brought him a small iron pot of paint and a brush. "I will paint you for the dance," he said.

He painted Goose Face first. Blue crescents on forehead, cheeks and chin, and a cross on the nose between the eyes. This paint was different than that which Sitting Bull himself wore, as his face was painted red, green and white. His hands and wrists were painted yellow and green. Will supposed that his being a medicine man and not a dancer explained the difference.

When he had finished with Goose Face, he painted Red Bird, and then crossed to Will. Will wanted to protest, yet some wisdom older than his nineteen years stopped the protest in his throat. His friends must not guess that he did not believe, even if he had to dance the Ghost Dance himself.

Goose Face and Red Bird left the lodge of Sitting Bull and moved toward the circle of dancers. Will followed, trying not to appear as reluctant as he felt. He noticed that many women were taking part and that each of them wore a single, pure white feather in her hair. This was unusual for until now dances had been reserved for men.

In the centre of the ring of dancers stood a tall pole with all sorts of flags and coloured cloth flying from it. Will guessed that the pole was symbolic of the one used for the Sun Dance before that dance had been forbidden by the whites.

This dance must have been going on continuously for several days. Many of the participants seemed to be in a state of near-exhaustion. Several lay motionless upon the ground.

Those who were still moving, moved in a single direction around the pole. When they would become too dizzy to continue in one direction, all would reverse direction and go the other way.

Goose Face moved into the circle and began to dance. Red Bird followed. Reluctantly, Will took his place behind Red Bird, knowing that if he did not want to earn the distrust and suspicion of his friends he must.

The dance was barbaric and childish. Yet as he danced, Will felt a strange excitement possessing him. His blood beat hard and fast through his body. His senses seemed to sharpen and a savage exaltation possessed him.

Ahead of him, Red Bird shrieked wildly and jumped up and down in a near frenzy.

Puzzled, Will realised that the dance was a thing of feeling, of the spirit rather than of the mind. Time seemed to lose meaning to him. Weariness and dizziness began to claim his body. He danced on, determined that in this, as in all other things, he would become part of the Sioux.

He was surprised when fires winked in the gathering darkness around the circle, when the spectators began to prepare their evening meal. Full darkness came down, and one by one the fires died.

Night passed and dawn came, grey and cold across the plain. The sun came up, without warmth, yet Will and the others danced on.

The smell of food came to him on the frosty morning breeze. He was hungry, but he knew he could not eat.

All day they danced, and now Will's mind was numb. His body felt like lead. He moved slowly, heavily, almost as though he were in a trance. The sun, warming as the day progressed, beat upon his back and he began to sweat. The blue face paint ran into his eyes and across his cheeks.

One by one, the dancers collapsed to the ground, unconscious. There they would remain, sometimes for several hours. But when one would awaken and rise, there would be, in his face, awe and fear and wonder. And Will wondered what he himself, an unbeliever, would dream when his turn came.

He danced harder, anxious now that it would be over soon. Many of the others flung stone tomahawks into the air, and sometimes someone was struck by one as it descended.

Goose Face went down, and Red Bird, and at

last Will himself stumbled and fell. It was good to lie upon the ground. His head whirled and bright lights flashed before his eyes. And suddenly he was conscious of nothing.

He lay this way for more than an hour. Then he began to stir and groan faintly.

He saw, not the face of Wakan Tanka, as the others did. He saw, instead, what he believed in his mind would come out of this desperation of the Sioux.

There was a wide plain and he stood on the edge of it, naked, without weapons, unable to intervene. At one side of the plain the Sioux were massed, sunlight gleaming from their bronzed and naked chests, and flashing from the brightness of warbonnets and weapons which, as they prepared to charge, they held above their heads.

At the other end of the plain were the whites, stolid and unimaginative in their heavy greatcoats, waiting. Ten thousand rifles turned their muzzles toward the Sioux. A thousand cannon stared and waited with huge and empty eyes.

Across the valley came the Sioux, screaming their war cries, singing their songs of battle and of death. When they were close enough the rifles chattered and the cannon roared.

Great clouds of powder smoke nearly obscured the whites and their armament. But nothing obscured the dying of the Sioux. The plain turned red, and rivers of blood ran across it. The bodies of horses lay scattered grotesquely and among them lay the dying Sioux.

Not one man escaped. Not one reached the ranks of massed Longknives.

And then, in the wake of the smoke and blood and noise, came another sound, a low wailing, a dirge from the far distance beyond the place from which the Sioux warriors had come. And Will saw the women crossing the plain afoot, searching among the dead. The sound of their mourning grew in his ears until he thought his sanity was leaving him.

He awoke with a violent start. Chilled to the bone, as much by the terror of his dream as by the cold, he lay still for a moment. Then he got up and staggered toward the fire nearest him.

He crouched over it, shivering violently. He noticed that several members of Sitting Bull's band looked at him strangely and went quickly away from him as though they were afraid.

Numb and exhausted as he was, he realised that the things he had dreamed were in his face. Because his expression showed none of the exaltation apparent in the others, it puzzled and frightened them.

He looked around for his friends. Goose Face still lay where he had fallen. He was covered with a blanket which some squaw had laid over him. Red Bird squatted beside an open fire nearby, eating from a bowl.

Will walked stiffly toward him. He saw in Red Bird's face the same wonder he had seen in the faces of others who had awakened while he danced.

A squaw gave him food and he ate ravenously. Red Bird asked, "Did you see him, Good Eagle?"

Will nodded, knowing Red Bird would never ask him to relate what he had seen.

They ate, and slept again, and early the following morning started back toward home. Goose Face had awakened while they slept, and had eaten too. Then he had slept beside them in the lodge of Sitting Bull.

Riding with them he said, "I have decided what I must do."

Will waited, and Goose Face went on. "I must stand with the Sioux, whether it be in fighting or in peace. It is what the Messiah has told me. Fight if you must, but only if you are driven to it."

It was what he wanted to believe, Will realised. It was the course he would eventually have chosen, with or without the help of the Ghost Dance and the fake Messiah. All Will himself could do was follow the dictates of his conscience.

His father was half-white and when the showdown came, he would stand solidly with the whites. Not because he wholly approved, nor because he was unsympathetic with the plight of the Sioux. Only because he felt he must.

Just as Will now felt he must stand on the side of the Sioux. Even if doing so meant losing his family and his life.

CHAPTER THREE

A dozen miles short of Pine Ridge Agency, Will left Goose Face and Red Bird and angled east toward home.

Home was a two-story frame ranch house surrounded by corrals and outbuildings. A single, enormous cottonwood shaded the yard, and behind the house, where a small creek ran, there was brush and trees of several varieties.

A certain unwilling nervousness touched Will as he approached. He had been gone for several days and his father would have guessed long before this where he had gone.

He rode into the yard and saw his father step out of the house and come toward him.

Luke Jordanais was a tall man, taller than Will by an inch. He wore his black, straight hair cut short. A few grey hairs were visible at his temples.

He was clean shaven, though his heavy beard was visible as a blue shadow across his jaws. He was dressed as any white rancher might be dressed.

Yet in spite of the way he looked and lived, there was much of the Indian about him. It showed itself in his dark skin, in his careful, watchful eyes, in his strong, wide mouth and in his nose, which was like the beak of a hawk. It showed itself in the way he walked and rode a horse.

In another time, Luke Jordanais would have been a scout for the Army, or a chief among the Sioux or Cheyenne. Perhaps by living as he did now, he was trying in his own small way to show the Indians that it could be done.

He frowned when he saw the streaks of blue on Will's face. He said, "For God's sake, I thought you had better sense than that!"

Meeting his glance steadily was not the easiest thing Will had ever done. He said, "I have. But I was with Goose Face and Red Bird. They believe in it and I had more sense than to scoff at them."

Luke's eyes sharpened as they studied his son. "So you danced. What did you find out?"

"That a man dreams what he wants to dream."

His father nodded, still studying him closely. "You've decided something. You've made up your mind. What are you going to do?"

"I want to marry Siya-Ka. I want to live with the Sioux."

An obscure sadness touched Luke's eyes. "Why don't you just sleep with her? You don't have to marry into the tribe."

Will felt a touch of anger that disappeared almost immediately. "I have known her since I was ten years old. I want more than to sleep with her."

For a moment they stared at each other, like two antagonists, each weighing the determination of the other. Then Will's father grunted reluctantly, "All right. I guess I've seen this coming for a long, long time. You're old enough to know what you want. But you're wrong. You're buying a hell of a lot of trouble for yourself."

"Three fourths of me is Indian. Only a fourth is white," Will said.

"That don't mean nothin'. The time ain't far off when they're all going to have to live like whites or be wiped out. And this damned fake Messiah isn't helping them any."

"Why not?" Will felt an inconsistent desire to defend the man. "He's giving them something they need. He's not telling them to do anything bad. He tells them to live good lives and not to fight the whites. Some ways his teachings are like those of the white man's Christ."

"So?"

"The white men accused their Christ of being a faker and nailed him to a cross."

Reluctant respect gleamed in Luke Jordanais's eyes. "You argue for him but you don't believe in him any more than I do. You know he's only something that grew out of the Indian's death struggle. He couldn't exist if the Indians weren't so desperate."

Will didn't reply because what his father had said was true.

Jordanais went on, "He's telling them what they want to hear that the tribes will grow strong again, that the buffalo will roam the plain in millions as they once did. Only it's impossible. The Indian is dying and the buffalo are dead. You'll die too if you insist on going to live with them."

"I will need horses for gifts to Red Bird. Will you give them to me?"

The father stared at Will helplessly. "You sure as hell got your mind made up, haven't you?"

Will nodded.

His father grinned suddenly without enthusiasm. "All right. Whatever horses you want are yours. Only pick the best. You don't want Red Bird to think you ain't properly respectful of his sister."

Will grinned back with relief. His father put a hand on his shoulder. "I'll take the horses to Red Bird myself." He hesitated a moment, then he said, "Half of me is Cheyenne so I'll tell you what an Indian father would tell his son. I'm proud of you because you're behavin' like a man even if you are all wrong. You're going to have to fight, so just fight like hell when the time for it comes."

Will's eyes burned and he gripped his father's hand. Suddenly his arms went out and he embraced his father. He turned away quickly, forcing steadiness into his voice. "I may be wrong like you say, but you'll never have to be ashamed of me."

"I know it. Come on up to the house and tell your mother what you're goin' to do. Then we'll get busy and gather some horses for you."

Will followed his father to the house. He shed his filthy clothing and bathed in the big galvanised tub his silent mother placed in the centre of the kitchen floor and filled for him.

She was tall, even for a Sioux woman. Her forehead came to Will's cheek. Dressed to-day in a white woman's calico dress, she wore her hair in braids, Indian fashion. This contrast, Will thought, was symbolic of the confusion in her heart. She was like a fish on land, belonging neither to the fish nor to the land creatures.

Among the whites she was considered Indian. Among the Indians she was considered white, or at least of the whites because she was married to a man half-white and because she lived in a white man's house.

Her calm face was engraved with deep lines of sadness, particularly noticeable to-day as though she had guessed what Will meant to do.

Bathing, Will watched her thoughtfully. He remembered nights when the three were together and alone, isolated by storm. Only on such nights had his mother ever seemed truly happy. She would cook fried bread for them which they ate with maple syrup called can-janpi-zizi by the

Sioux or "yellow juice of the wood" and they would afterward sing some of the ancient songs of the Sioux.

Nor was his father any happier. He shared his wife's loneliness, living neither wholly in the white man's world nor in that of the Indian. Instead he lived in a strange half-world which was part Indian and part white.

That, Will thought, may have been what attracted him to the Sioux. With them he had found the acceptance he needed. He had known, perhaps, that he would never find it among the whites.

He spoke to his mother in the tongue of the Sioux. "I have chosen a bride. To-morrow Father and I will begin to gather horses as a gift to her brother."

She stopped and stood motionless, her back to him, and he went on, "The girl is Siya-Ka, sister of Red Bird, in the village of Goose Face."

Still she stood motionless. Will got out of the tub and began to dry his powerful body. At last she turned. There were tears in her eyes as she glanced from Will to his father and back again. "Trouble is coming," she said. "Your father is of the whites and will fight with them. How can you fight against him?"

"I will never fight against him," Will replied. "Nor will he fight against me."

Tears spilled from her eyes and ran across her

cheeks. Will's father went to her and put an arm around her shoulders.

Will felt ashamed because he had saddened her. Yet he sensed that in her heart she approved of what he had done.

He dressed quickly and hurried out. He saddled horses for himself and for his father. By the time he had finished, he saw his father crossing the yard toward the corral. They mounted and rode out together toward the north.

They talked little as they rode. Their minds and thoughts were now upon gathering a herd of the best horses on the ranch as quickly as they could.

Three days were consumed in gathering the herd. Still not satisfied, Will's father sent him to the trader's store at Pine Ridge to buy a new Winchester repeating rifle for Red Bird. It was almost a week after Will's return from the village of Sitting Bull that Luke Jordanais set out, driving the horses toward the village of Goose Face.

Will watched him go worriedly. He had no assurance that Red Bird would accept the gifts. Acceptance as a friend is one thing. Acceptance as a relative is quite another.

He began to work at repairing the corral, driving himself so that the time would pass quickly, so that he would not worry about whether Red Bird would accept the gift. But he could not keep his thoughts from seeing Siya-Ka, nor could he keep from wanting her.

The day dragged past. Night came, frosty and cold. Will ate supper, then went out to stand in the cold wind, staring toward the southwest. His father should have reached Goose Face's village by now, he thought. His father should know what Red Bird's answer was.

He considered riding out and trying to intercept his father, but he didn't move. He might miss his father in the darkness.

He tensed suddenly. He strained his ears, listening . . .

And he heard it again—a sound, faint with distance. He ran eagerly in the direction of the sound.

Before he had cleared the yard, he heard the steady pound of a horse's hooves. A moment later, the shadowy shape of a horse and rider loomed out of the dark.

The horse pulled up, plunging, as he reached Will. The man riding him fell from the saddle and hit the ground with a sodden thump.

Elation gone, dismay touching him, Will knelt. Faint light from the winter stars reflected from Luke Jordanais's sweaty face. Even in this light, Will could see how grey it was. He could also see the feathered shaft of the arrow that protruded from his father's back.

Will slid his arms beneath his father, lifted him

bodily, and carried him toward the house at a shuffling trot.

His mind seethed with mingled fury and puzzlement. Who had done this? Red Bird? Goose Face? But why? A man may refuse gifts but he does not attack the man who offers them.

The door of the house opened and light streamed out of it. Will carried his father in and laid him, face down, on his bed. His mother watched with little noticeable change of expression and no tears. Only her pallor, only the terrible pain in her eyes revealed her concern.

Without hesitation, she straddled her husband's body and grasped the arrow firmly in both hands. With a sudden jerk, she yanked it free. Blood gushed in its wake.

Will could think of nothing but that his father was going to die, that his killers would escape. Luke Jordanais might never speak again, might never be able to tell anyone who they were.

Will's mother put compresses on the wound to absorb the blood. Then she turned her head and looked at Will. "I will care for him. You must find the ones who did this and punish them."

Will nodded.

She said warningly, "It is a Sioux arrow. If . . ."

Will's face twisted suddenly and his eyes blurred with tears. "It will not matter," he said harshly.

Will turned and stumbled out the door. He

went to his father's horse standing where Luke Jordanais had fallen from his back. He picked up the Winchester his father had been carrying. Checking it, he found that it was loaded.

Hurrying, he led the horse to the corral where he changed the saddle and bridle to a fresh horse. He mounted and rode out at a gallop in the direction from which his father had come.

How long Luke Jordanais had lain unconscious after he had been shot, Will didn't know. But he must have been shot a long distance from home.

Patches of snow lay here and there upon the plains. Using only direction and an occasional trail through a patch of snow, visible even in poor starlight, Will stubbornly followed his father's trail.

And riding, he realised that this was the beginning of the end for him. Siya-Ka could never belong to him now.

He would catch and kill the man who had shot his father. He would kill a Sioux, perhaps even one from the village of Goose Face, who also wanted Siya-Ka.

Red Bird could never accept his gifts after that. The lines would be too plainly drawn. Who kills a Sioux takes his place on the side of the whites, no matter what the reason for his deed. He could not be both Sioux and white.

But he didn't hesitate. His eyes, trained by none other than Goose Face himself, read his father's trail unerringly in spite of the darkness and the difficulty.

It was after midnight when he came to the place where his father had been shot. He stopped, moved slowly ahead, and circled carefully.

Three men had participated in the attack. A spent arrow, lying on the ground, testified to the fact that their first shot had missed.

They had taken the horses and had ridden away as fast as they could travel. They had headed southwest along a course that, if continued, would miss Pine Ridge Indian Agency by more than ten miles.

Will frowned. Why hadn't they driven the horses toward the badlands? Or why not toward the north, where it would be so much easier to stay hidden as they rode?

The answer seemed simple enough. They had not counted on Luke Jordanais's tremendous vitality. They had thought him mortally wounded, had thought his death would not be discovered for at least a day.

Will had never hunted men before. He would have been lying if he had said he was not afraid. Yet his fury and his outrage dwarfed his fear. To-night he was a Sioux warrior, on the warpath for perhaps the first and the last time in his life.

All through the night he rode, faster than before because the trail of the driven horses was easier to follow than the trail of his father's horse, yet still not so fast as the horse thieves had driven the band. He was grateful when the eastern sky began to turn cold grey, grateful when the light increased enough so that he could push his horse to the limit of his strength.

He thought of Siya-Ka, who now was undoubtedly lost to him. He thought of his friends in the village of Goose Face, and wondered which of them he must kill to-day.

A wind came up in the north and blew its icy breath across the plain. The sky misted and partly hid the sun, without warmth this early in the day.

And always the trail led south and west, toward the strip of land in northern Nebraska which Spotted Tail had traded to the whites a decade before.

Realisation of the thieves' destination brought a frown of puzzlement to Will's face. There, in that strip of land, lived the wolves that fed upon the Sioux nation. Here were the whites who bought at ridiculous prices the clothing and blankets and wagons which the government gave to the Sioux, or who traded whisky for them. Border cut-throats and renegades of all descriptions. Horse thieves and cattle rustlers. Murderers and gamblers, all preying upon Sioux.

Will drew his horse to a halt. The tracks of one horse abruptly left the other and angled straight toward Pine Ridge Indian Agency.

Will hesitated indecisively. Should he follow the single rider, who had left his companions? Or should he follow the two and the band of stolen horses?

If he followed the two, he might lose the single rider altogether, for the man would lose his tracks either at Pine Ridge or in some Indian village nearby.

On the other hand, if he followed the single rider, he might be lucky enough to catch him quickly and be able to return his attention to the other two.

He turned his horse and kicked him into a run again. He followed the single trail.

The air kept getting colder as he rode. The overcast grew heavier until the sun became but a faintly glowing ball in the sky, a ball which looked a great deal like a pale, white moon.

Grey clouds began to pile up on the northern horizon. He was grateful that he had taken time to get a heavy sheepskin coat and red woollen gloves before he had left home.

Warm fingers would be needed to operate the Winchester. Warm fingers and a body that did not tremble with the cold.

A flake of snow stung his face. And then another. Before he had gone three miles from the forked trail, the air was filled with driving flakes.

He urged his horse to even greater speed, feeling now a frantic fear that he would lose his quarry in the storm. Already the tracks were beginning to fade and become covered with the snow.

He climbed a bluff, still closely following trail, doing so at a fast trot, for the tracks were hard to see. He crested the bluff and saw where his quarry had paused to look back along his trail.

Will knew the man could not have missed seeing him, and a sudden wariness touched him. Even now the man might be hidden within range aiming his arrow at Will's chest.

But he couldn't stop, or even slow down. He could only go on, as fast as he could, trying to catch the man before the snow obliterated his trail. Anyway, the thief might well miss with his first shot as he had missed his first shot at Will's father. And if he did, Will would know where he had concealed himself.

He had prepared himself for an arrow, but not for a gun. It was with complete surprise that he heard the unmistakable sound of a bullet striking flesh and the barest instant later, the loud report of a gun.

The first fleeting thought that crossed his mind was that the bullet had struck him. Then his horse faltered and went to his knees. Will flung himself clear and the horse collapsed quietly, to lie upon his side.

Again the rifle roared. Will leaped across his horse's body and flung himself prone on the other side. He slid the Winchester forward and rested it upon the horse's sweaty, foam-flecked belly.

Blood welled from a gaping hole in the horse's shoulder, but it was already beginning to clot in the icy air. The horse was dead.

Will felt a sense of loss. He felt a sense of terrible aloneness. His father's words came back to him. "You will have to fight. Fight well when that time comes."

He knew his enemy's hiding place. He had spotted it from the cloud of black smoke that had belched from the ambusher's gun. He wondered now who the man would be. A Brule? A Yanktonais? One of the Ogalallas, perhaps even one from Goose Face's village? Or a white?

He caught movement in the brush-screened gully where the ambusher had concealed himself. He snapped a quick shot at it even as he saw that it was a wide-brimmed high-crowned hat.

The hat meant nothing. It was the kind issued to the Sioux along with the heavy greatcoats which few of them would wear. It was a hat worn both by Indians and by whites.

A blinding flurry of snow descended between Will and his quarry, blotting out the brush in which the man was hidden.

Will didn't think, or hesitate. He leaped to his feet, crouching instinctively as he ran. He did not head directly toward the man, but instead made a wide half circle so that he might come upon his enemy from the side.

His face was soaked from melting snow and his rifle was white with the huge flakes that had accumulated on it. How long it took him to reach the cover of the brushy gully, he couldn't have said. It seemed forever, but it could scarcely have been more than half a minute.

He caught a blur of black before him, which materialised almost immediately into the half-concealed prone body of a man.

Anger, which had died to smouldering coals during the long ride, now flared anew in Will. He experienced a wild, killing fury.

Gone, suddenly, was the white training his mind had absorbed. Presently in him now was the heritage of a thousand generations of Indian wanderers, primitive, savage. He was like the great mountain cat leaping upon his unsuspecting kill. He flung his rifle up and snapped a shot at the man's prone body.

The bullet struck. The man had no time to rise. But he rolled, and brought his own gun to bear on Will.

Will was too close to fire again. Instead, he brought his rifle slamming against the muzzle of the other's gun and swept it aside. In that instant, he saw clearly the man who had shot his father. This was no Indian, but a white, evil-looking, with a week's growth of reddish whiskers on his face.

Will would remember those eyes until the day he died. They were pale grey, and cold as the winter sky.

The man fought to bring his gun to bear again. Will saw, lying beside him, a Sioux bow and a quiver of Sioux arrows.

Sight of them drove away whatever restraint might have remained in him. He clubbed his rifle with a single, swift movement, and brought it swinging toward the other's head.

Panic flashed in those evil eyes. The man's mouth sagged open, loose lipped, to reveal a mouthful of crooked, yellow teeth. He tried to raise his rifle and fend off Will's blow.

He might as well have tried to stop it with his hands. Will heard the stock of the man's rifle splinter as his own rifle struck it. Then he heard the sodden crack of the rifle stock against the other's head. The man was driven back until his body sprawled across the bow and the quiver of arrows. He lay completely still.

No longer did his chest rise and fall with his breathing. The only sign that there once had been life in him was a twitching muscle in his cheek.

Will stood over him, breathing hard. His enemy was dead. He had met, fought, and defeated him. He had killed for the first time.

His feelings were confused. The man had been a human being. Will felt a contradictory sense of loss, for life had been taken and could never be restored.

Overriding this feeling, however, was another, which came to him from generations of Sioux and Cheyenne. He felt pride, for he had counted a coup and had proved himself a man.

He did not know how long he stood there in the driving snow and chilling wind. Long enough for his face to become covered with slushy flakes. Long enough for his sweating body to chill.

One thing yet remained to be done. His father, if he still lived, must see proof that he had been avenged before he died.

Will had never seen a scalp taken, though he had seen many scalps and had heard many tales of exactly how it was done. You grasped the hair firmly in the left hand. With the right, you made a quick, circular incision in the scalp.

Will drew his knife with hands that trembled. He tested its blade, which was nearly keen enough to shave with. He bent over his fallen enemy. And he hesitated, restrained momentarily by his white training and early environment.

He knew that scalping was not an Indian custom in origin. It was taught to the Indians by the Wasicunhin-ca, the French, who were the first whites to invade the land of the Sioux. They paid a bounty on the scalps of Englishmen.

But the Sioux had embraced the custom willingly, for it provided proof of the counting of a coup.

Suddenly Will bent, grasped the greasy hair of the white man firmly in his left hand. With his right, he made the swift incision.

Strangely enough, it was like skinning a deer. He felt nothing. No revulsion. No shame or regret. This was only a dead thing, containing nothing of the human spirit which had so recently dwelt in it.

Will turned and walked away. He searched in the driving storm until he had found the white renegade's horse. He mounted and rode away, with the horse turning his head in fear because of the smell of blood.

He had not ridden a mile in the direction of home before he realised that he could not keep the scalp. His father would not want to see it.

He stared down at it. It seemed like nothing, not a symbol of victory, not proof of his kill. It was only a piece of hair and flesh, of no more importance than a piece of deer hide. He released his grip on it and it fell into the snow. Briefly, it was a black spot there and then he was past and it was gone.

He bent his head against the force of the storm and dug his heels into the horse's sides.

No use trying to return and pick up the trail of the other two. It would be completely hidden by the storm.

Will did not consider what the consequences of the killing would be. He did not consider what discovery of the white man's body would do to the already uneasy whites.

The man's head was scalped and his horse was gone. There was no evidence to prove that he had been a horse thief, or that he had shot Will's father in the commission of a crime.

One conclusion only could be drawn by the whites when the man's body was brought in. Hostilities had begun. The Sioux nation had begun to rise.

CHAPTER FOUR

The storm swirled around Will as he rode, blotting out everything more than half a dozen yards away.

It was as though he rode in a void, above the earth, where there was neither sound nor sight nor smell.

His concern for his father was great and he wondered if his father still lived or not. But he was nearly halfway home before he began to consider the consequences of what had happened to-day.

The white man he had killed and scalped would be found. That was a certainty. His comrades would miss him and would search for him.

The killings would, of course, be blamed upon the Sioux. Nor would the whites bother to hunt down the single man responsible. Instead, they would blame all Sioux.

This, thought Will, was one of the sources of everlasting conflict between Indian and white. Nor were the whites the only ones guilty of it. The Indians too blamed any bad thing done by a white upon all whites.

Vengeance, then, was taken for any wrong upon the nearest available member of the other race. And vengeance for that wrong, in turn, taken upon someone else.

Such a practice inevitably led to conflict and more conflict. Perhaps Indian and white could never live in peace. Not until every Indian had been exterminated.

Ten miles from home, Will kicked the horse into a sluggish trot. It was still snowing heavily. An accumulation of several inches lay upon the frozen ground.

He dismounted at the door and hurried into the house. His mother sat in a chair, dozing. Her eyes opened as he came in.

He did not have to speak. The terrible question was in his eyes.

She said, "He lives."

Will crossed the room and went into the bedroom where his father was. He had never seen his father's face so grey, so drawn. He watched the slow, laboured breathing for a moment.

His father still lived. But for how long? Will felt something icy in his chest. He turned and went back to where his mother was. "The man who shot him is dead," he said.

She did not seem to hear. He stared at her for a moment, then went out again into the snow. He removed saddle and bridle from the horse and turned the animal loose. The horse lay down and rolled, then got up and disappeared into the storm.

He crossed to the barn and went inside. He paced back and forth, frowning.

Weariness was strong in him. At last he lay down upon a pile of hay and went to sleep.

Hoofbeats awoke him. He went outside into the storm and saw three uniformed Indian police riding in. He crossed the yard to them warily.

Their leader, heavy-set, dark of face, said hoarsely, "We want to see Luke Jordanais."

"He's been hurt."

"How?"

"An arrow in the back. He is unconscious."

The Indian policeman said, "We are warning everyone to leave the reservation. You had better leave and take him with you."

"Why?"

"There is trouble. The Sioux may rise. A scalped white man was brought in only hours ago, and the white soldiers are too few to protect everyone. There are less than fifteen hundred of them and there are six thousand Sioux warriors at Pine Ridge and Rosebud Agencies. Six hundred of them are dancing the Ghost Dance at Little Wound's camp not more than fifteen miles from here and they are all armed."

"We can't leave," Will said. "The journey would kill my father."

"You have been warned," the man said. He spoke to his companions and the trio rode away.

Will stared after them. He could imagine the terror in Rushville, and at Pine Ridge and Rosebud Agencies. The whites would be thinking of the massacres in Minnesota in 1862. They would be thinking of the seven hundred killed in less than a week's time.

The Agencies would be guarded twenty-four hours a day. Cannon and Gatling guns would have been emplaced. Troops would be moving all over the Dakotas and there would be other incidents.

It was now growing dark. Will went into the house. His mother was cooking supper. "Is he better?" he asked.

"He is conscious." Her face was impassive, but there was a sparkle in her eyes that had not been there before.

Will went quietly into his father's room. He was appalled at the way his father looked—as though he had lost forty pounds in as many hours.

His voice was weak and thin. "Did you recover the horses?"

Will shook his head. "But I overtook one of the men—the one who shot you. He was a white man and he is dead."

Luke Jordanais nodded weakly. "I'm sorry about the horses."

Will did not reply, and after a moment his father went on. "Don't ever admit you killed that man. He was white and you are mostly Indian. They'd try you for it in their courts and you'd find no justice there."

"Would it do any good to go to Rushville and

report the horses stolen?" Will asked. "Would there be any chance of getting them back?"

"You can try." He closed his eyes and lay very still. The covers over him rose and fell with his deep, painful breathing.

Will went out and found his mother standing just outside the door. She said softly, "The arrow missed his lungs and heart. He was lucky."

"Will he be all right?" Will asked.

"I have prayed to the God of the Sioux and to the God of the white men." Her dark eyes were steady and inscrutable on Will's face. He had never been able to guess her thoughts and he could not now. Yet he could not doubt her love for his father.

She was as so many among the Sioux were, neither white nor wholly Indian. She had given up the Indian ways for those of the whites. Yet she did not understand the whites and so was lost, secure only in her love for Will's father.

Will didn't know what she would do if his father died. She couldn't go to live among the whites, for there was no place for her there. Nor could she return to the Sioux, for so doing would be a betrayal of her husband and of the things in which he believed. She probably would die herself before many months had passed.

The storm was beginning to clear as Will went outside again. Before he had gone five miles, the sun came out, bright and warm.

Six inches of snow lay on the ground. The sun hung close to the western horizon, growing red as it sank slowly toward the earth.

Will pushed his horse steadily, but even so it was late when he arrived.

Rushville was a booming frontier town of about twelve hundred inhabitants, and it was apparent, even to Will, that the town was as uncertain as the Sioux, trying to decide whether it was to be of the East or of the West.

The town lay mostly on a single street, at right angles to the railroad track. A train had just come in and from the station came a weary stream of passengers, heading upstreet toward the hotels and saloons. A detachment of soldiers marched from the station toward an Army encampment at the edge of town.

Mud, inches deep in the street, was kept churned up constantly by an unending stream of horsemen, buggies, and freight wagons. It always froze at night, and each morning was roughened so that wagons and other rigs made a loud clatter passing over it.

Will had been to Rushville with his father, so he was no stranger to it. But it was different to-night. A woman glanced at him with fright in her eyes. A buffalo hunter a dozen feet behind her, bearded and dirty, glared at him challengingly.

Will realised that even in his white man's clothes he looked more Indian than white. He had the long, straight nose of the Sioux, the dark complexion, the black eyes and straight, wide mouth. And he was tall, like most Sioux warriors, taller than the average white.

Other things of which he was not aware may have contributed to the impression that he was Indian—the way he sat his horse, the muscular strength and power of his body.

But he felt the tension in the town the moment he rode into it. There was fear, so strong it made his neck tingle. There was uneasiness and the knowledge that if the Sioux decided to sack and burn the town, to murder its inhabitants, nothing existed that could stop them.

All the men went armed. Will saw one man, with handsome, greying sideburns, dressed in a grey broadcloth suit and wearing a derby hat. About his waist was strapped a cartridge belt and revolver. Others carried rifles and some, shotguns.

An unpleasant, unhealthy, dangerous atmosphere, that made Will feel uneasy himself. He rode directly to the grey stone building that housed the sheriff's office and the jail.

The man at the desk was oldish, with a white, cavalry-style moustache and an unshaven chin. As Will came in, he spat tobacco juice at a spittoon beside the desk and missed.

"I want to report some horses stolen and I want you to get them back," Will said.

The man stared at him with hard, unfriendly eyes. "Injun, ain't ye?"

"I am half-Sioux, one-fourth Cheyenne and one-fourth white."

"Breed, huh?" The man made no effort to conceal his contempt.

Will's eyes narrowed with anger. "Both Indian and whites are supposed to be under the protection of the white man's laws. My father has been shot and our horses stolen. I want them back."

"What's your name?"

"Jordanais. Will Jordanais."

"Oh yeah. Your old man got a Sioux arrow in the back, didn't he?"

Will started to protest, to say the arrow had been shot by a white. Then he stopped.

The man at the desk shrugged with sudden unconcern. "That makes it none of my business. Makes it the business of the Indian Bureau. You go on over to Pine Ridge and tell the agent your troubles."

"What if the thieves were white?"

"Was they?" The man's eyes sharpened.

"My father thought they were," Will said.

The man shook his head. "Don't hold water. Don't make sense. It ain't the whites that's stirrin' things up, it's them murderin' bucks. An' you folks bein' half-breeds makes you fair game for them. Tell the agent about it. Don't bother me."

"But . . ."

"Git outa here now. Git!"

Will started at him furiously. The man's hand edged almost imperceptibly toward the shotgun leaning against the desk an arm's length away.

Will swung around and went out. Little wonder the Sioux were rebellious. The laws were supposed to protect Indian and whites equally, yet they did not. Had Will been white, he would have been asked to sit down and would have been listened to courteously. The deputy would have taken a description of the horses. The Agency Indian Police would have been notified and in time the horses would have been returned.

Thoroughly angered, he galloped out of town. It was growing light when he reached Pine Ridge.

As he rode toward the buildings, a soldier with a rifle challenged him. Will called out his name and the man motioned him to come closer.

The guard stared up at him for a moment. Then he said, "Breed, ain't you? Lemme tell you, boy, you better make tracks. The damn' Sioux don't like breeds much better'n they do us whites. An' there's plenty of trouble comin' in a day or two. Soon as them soldiers General Miles sent to Grand River get their hands on Sittin' Bull."

The man seemed to want to talk. He went on, "Way I hear it, General Miles don't want the damn' renegade taken alive. So the Indian police will kill him if they can."

Will whirled his horse disgustedly and rode

away. There was little point in complaining to the agent about the stolen horses anyway. At a time like this, nothing would be done.

Riding, he wondered at the foolishness of what General Miles had ordered done. If they killed Sitting Bull . . .

The members of his band would ride out, in all directions, with the news. In twenty-four hours every Sioux in the Dakotas would know that he was dead.

Already frightened and bewildered—already believing in their hearts that the white men wished to exterminate them—they would rise, and fight. They would believe the time had come when the white men wanted what little was left of their lands. Pine Ridge, Rosebud, Standing Rock. They would believe that the reduction of the beef allotment was deliberate—to weaken them so that the soldiers could come among them and slaughter them like steers.

And maybe that was what the whites did intend, thought Will. He remembered Sitting Bull's words: "What treaty have the whites made that they have kept. Not one."

The words were true. The whites had bargained the Black Hills from the Sioux, promising in return three pounds of beef a day to each Indian forever. Had they kept that promise? Had they even tried to keep it?

Will was young, and he had heard many tales

of the battles of the past. He could not help the way his blood raced at the thought of new battles in which he might participate.

He passed a small party of Indian police, and asked them where the band of Goose Face was encamped. Guided by the directions he received from them, he rode directly toward it.

Goose Face's small band was encamped with perhaps a dozen others, all comprising the larger band of Big Foot, the chief who had so narrowly averted a dangerous incident during the beef issue a week before.

A Ghost Dance was in progress, in which almost a hundred men and women were participating. Will didn't linger to watch, but rode quickly through the village looking for the tepees of Goose Face and Red Bird.

Nearly all the Indians Will passed looked at him suspiciously. A few muttered. One or two seemed close to challenging him.

All of them knew him. Yet now they felt distrust, for they knew his father was half-white and lived as did the whites. They suspected him of being a spy.

At the far edge of the encampment, he found the tepee of Red Bird. Red Bird came out of his lodge as Will approached. His forehead, cheeks, and chin were painted with blue crescents. On the bridge of his nose was a blue cross. He was preparing to join the Ghost Dance and Will knew that once he did, there would be no further chance to talk to him for several days.

"I would speak with you, Red Bird," Will said. "I have spent many days gathering the best of our horses as a gift to you. White men stole them and shot my father, who was delivering them. Even now, he lies near to death."

He was surprised at the expression in Red Bird's eyes. They held no friendliness, but were impassive and inscrutable. He grunted, "I would not have accepted horses from Will Jordanais anyway."

Will experienced a sinking sensation in his stomach. Red Bird had never called him by his Christian name before. For a moment he could not speak.

Red Bird's expression altered only slightly. He said, "You are of the whites, for all that you have tried to be one of us. You speak the white man's language and live in a white man's house. Many among us say you cannot be trusted, that you will betray us when the time for battle comes."

Reckless anger touched Will. His face lost colour and his eyes narrowed. He said harshly, "I would dispute that with whoever says I will betray my friends."

He thought Red Bird's eyes warmed slightly, but he could not be sure, for Red Bird's voice was still cold when he spoke. "Siya-Ka would not be happy in a white man's house. She would be as your mother is, neither of the whites nor of the Sioux. It is not good. She has need to belong."

"But I wish to live among the Sioux."

Impatience touched Red Bird's eyes at Will's argumentative tone. He said shortly, "There is no need to bring me gifts. I will not keep them."

It was refusal, adamant and final, and it brought back the reckless anger to Will's mind. He said fiercely, "Perhaps you have more liking for another's gifts. Perhaps that other is the one who says I cannot be trusted. If this is so, I will seek him out. We shall see if he fights as well as he talks."

Again he had the vague notion that Red Bird's eyes warmed. But refusal was still in the Indian's face. Red Bird said, "I go to dance the Ghost Dance. Return to me in three days with the gifts you wish to give. Then will the final decision be made." He turned his back and walked away.

Will wanted to follow him, to argue bitterly, to force consent from him. But he knew it was no use. A Sioux takes very seriously the responsibility which custom thrusts upon him. Besides that, Will knew the deep affection that existed between Siya-Ka and her brother, Red Bird.

He was only doing what he believed was right. And Will knew it was up to him to show Red Bird that he was wrong. If he failed . . .

The thought depressed him. If he failed, then Siya-Ka was forever lost to him.

The thought was intolerable. He could not bear to contemplate a life without her. He felt suddenly alone. Outcast from the Sioux, unaccepted by the whites, where would he go and what would he do?

Will became aware that he was being watched. Glancing toward the flap of Red Bird's tepee, he saw Siya-Ka peeping out from behind it. "You heard?" he said.

She nodded.

"Come out. I would talk with you," he said.

Siya-Ka pushed aside the flap and came out. She was dressed in her finest white deerskin, lavishly fringed and decorated, both with beads and with coloured porcupine quills. She stood, hesitant and unsmiling, just outside the flap.

Looking down at her, Will's heart beat faster. But there was pain in it too, pain in knowing she might belong to another and not to him. "Who is the one who has presented gifts to Red Bird?" he asked.

She did not answer immediately. Her great, dark eyes rested upon him, as though she were trying to decide something in her mind.

The fires near the Ghost Dance circle poured a thin smoke into the air, smoke that was fragrant as it drifted through the village. In Will's ears were the cries of the dancers.

Somewhere several dogs began to bark. A child cried, and was scolded by a squaw's shrill voice.

Familiar, friendly sounds. Yet somehow the village suddenly reminded Will of Rushville, which he had so recently left. For within it was the same fear and unease.

Siya-Ka spoke timidly: "It is Ptesan—White Buffalo—who has presented gifts to Red Bird. There were five horses, though two of them were thin."

Will could not resist a moment of boastfulness. "Twenty horses were to have been my gift to Red Bird. Twenty of my father's finest. I would not have it said that I did not hold Siya-Ka in high esteem. Now, with the best of the horses stolen, I will bring thirty of the next best." He didn't know whether he could find thirty horses in three days' time. He did know that he would exhaust himself trying.

Her eyes were proud and soft as they rested on him. Her full lips curved into a shy smile. A pulse beat in her throat, like the wings of a frightened bird. Her breasts rose and fell with her rapid breathing.

Her fright won. She whispered, "Do not touch me, Good Eagle. Red Bird would hear of it and would certainly return your gifts."

The blood was pounding in Will's brain. He touched her arm and would have seized it, but suddenly she broke away and disappeared into Red Bird's tepee.

He hesitated. He knew he could go in. There was no lock upon the door. He could go in and Siya-Ka would welcome him.

Yet suddenly he knew this was not the way he wanted it. He could envision her standing just inside, trembling, frightened, yet hopeful too.

He hesitated for a long, long time. Then, reluctantly, he turned away.

He knew he did not want her for a single night. He wanted her for the rest of his life. If he were to live among the Sioux, he must respect their customs and do things the way she did. Slipping into her tepee like a thief was not the way of the Sioux.

Sweating with his excitement and with his efforts to control himself, he mounted his horse.

Three days. It was all he had. And he would have no help in gathering the horses he had to have.

He dug his heels into his horse's sides and left the village at a run. Three days was not much time.

Even if he succeeded in gathering the horses, in driving them safely here, there was no guarantee Red Bird would accept them from him.

Desperation briefly touched his heart. If Red Bird said no, at least this Ptesan would not get Siya-Ka. Because Will would seek him out and kill him, even if his own life be forfeit for the killing. His face hard, his eyes narrowed with both anger and determination, he pounded at a steady gallop across the frozen plain.

CHAPTER FIVE

Will could not help being angry as he rode toward home. Angry at Red Bird, whose behaviour toward him had so suddenly and radically changed.

Less than a week ago he had ridden to Grand River with Red Bird and Goose Face and had danced the Ghost Dance with them at the camp of Sitting Bull. Red Bird had seemed to favour him then as a husband for his sister.

Now, apparently, he did not. He even seemed to suspect Will of being a spy for the whites. He had probably been listening to White Buffalo, who was undoubtedly doing his best to discredit Will.

Frowning, Will realised he could hardly blame Red Bird for his lack of faith. The past had certainly furnished plentiful grounds for suspicion. Hundreds of full-blooded Sioux had gone over to the whites. Some had become Indian police. Others, who had children at the Carlisle Indian School back east in Pennsylvania, spoke up staunchly for the whites because they feared their children would be killed if they did not. Still others, some of the Sioux chiefs among these, had accepted money from the whites in return for the so-called "scouting" services for their half-grown sons. In reality, this money was nothing more or less than a bribe to ensure the loyalty of the chiefs involved.

When Will reached home, it was very late. He put his horse away and hurried into the house.

There was a lamp burning in his father's room. He went to the door and saw that his father was awake.

There was more colour in Luke Jordanais's face to-night. "Any luck?" he asked.

Will shook his head. "They told me to see the Indian agent at Pine Ridge."

His father nodded. "I expected that but I didn't figure it would hurt to try. What are you going to do now?"

Will's jaw hardened stubbornly. "Gather more horses. Thirty this time, because the best are gone."

His father nodded. He stared for a moment at Will, then asked, "Things are worse, aren't they?"

Will nodded reluctantly. "General Miles has sent soldiers to arrest Sitting Bull. They do not really intend to arrest him but will kill him if they can."

"And the Sioux?"

"They're dancing the Ghost Dance. In every village. Red Bird was suspicious of me and I don't know if he'll accept the horses or not."

"And if he doesn't?"

"I'll stay with them anyway. I'll prove to them that I'm loyal to them."

His father closed his eyes, a troubled frown on his face. Will left the room and went to his own. A nearly impossible task faced him, but he would accomplish it. Siya-Ka and his life with her was at stake.

He was up before dawn and found his mother in the kitchen preparing breakfast for him. He sat down and gulped a cup of scalding coffee.

She put fried beef and fried bread in front of him without speaking. Her face held sadness and her eyes were filled with worry.

"It will be all right," Will said. "The Sioux will probably not fight the whites at all. It's winter and they never fight in winter. Just because they're dancing the Ghost Dance doesn't mean that they will fight."

"They will fight." Her voice was dead, without hope. "I have lived many winters. I have seen them fight many times. But it is always the same. The whites are too many for the Sioux and the Sioux are fools."

"Fools to fight for what is right?"

"What is right and what is wrong? There is right on both sides of every argument. And fighting will solve nothing. It never has."

Will didn't reply.

She went on. "Both the Sioux and the whites are children. They are afraid of each other. And when children are afraid they believe many lies."

He knew she was right. There were Sioux who believed the whites wanted every Indian in America dead. And whites who believed the Sioux could never change, that they would be bloodthirsty savages until they died.

Will finished his breakfast. He went out into the grey cold dawn and saddled a horse. He mounted and rode away to begin his search.

The land around the house was rolling, prairie country. Occasionally a bluff would rise from its comparatively level surface. Occasionally it would be cut by a wide, sandy stream bed or by a dry wash with precipitous sides.

It was a windy day and the gusts made the waving, dry-brown grass appear like winter, rippling and bending before its insistent force.

The sun came up. The thin overcast that lay across the sky had been turned brilliant pink earlier by the predawn rays of the sun but was now a cheerless grey that robbed the sun of its warmth.

Will sighted cattle, but no horses. He was not discouraged, however, since horses are not like cattle. They travel in a bunch and seldom separate to graze alone as cattle do. When he found horses he knew he would find many of them in one place.

It was afternoon before he sighted any and then

only a small bunch grazing on the top of a long bluff.

He circled the bluff, taking a full hour to do so, since he knew that to approach directly would be to drive them away from home in their first start of surprise when they sighted him.

He topped the bluff. Immediately one of the horses raised his head and trumpeted. The others turned to look, then galloped away, tails and manes bannering out in the wind.

He followed at a pace equal to theirs until they had streamed down off the bluff, leaving a towering, swift-travelling cloud of dust in their wake. Then he drummed on his horse's sides with his heels and let him run.

Not once did he close the gap between the horses and himself to less than a quarter-mile, yet each time they bore too much to left or right, he would ease over and edge them back to the proper course.

This way, he covered most of the ten miles to the ranch house at a hard run. When he came in sight of the buildings, the horses were tired enough to be corralled.

He made a wide circle and came in ahead of them to open the gate. Circling again, he drove them in.

He could remember many times in the past when he had been forced to work half a day or more corralling a small band of horses such as these. He heaved a sigh of relief.

He dismounted and led his horse to the barn. He fed him and selected another from the corral to ride. He rode out immediately.

At nightfall, he had a total catch of twenty-two, of which only seven were suitable for his gift to Red Bird. Weary and discouraged, he went into the house.

His mother gave him supper and his father encouragement. "To-morrow try the land to the west. There are a lot of grassy valleys in that direction where the horses like to stay this time of year. You'll probably find as many as you need."

Will could see that he didn't really believe his own words. He knew, and so did Will, that this job required more men.

But he had no intention of giving up. If he didn't have thirty of the kind of horses he wanted by the time the three days had passed, then he'd simply have to select the best thirty from among those he had. They would have to do.

He slept exhaustedly, and was up again the following day before dawn. Again he rode out, this time heading west as his father had suggested.

He worked all day at top speed. At nightfall, he had corralled twenty more. Nine were suitable for giving to Red Bird.

So he had sixteen. Only a little more than half the number he needed. And two-thirds of his time was gone.

He worked like a madman the following day. He wore out four horses. But at the end of the day he had twenty-six suitable horses and could fill in with four young mares.

In darkness, with his mother's help, he cut out the horses he didn't want and released them from the corral.

For several minutes he stood looking at those that remained approvingly. He felt a strong sense of satisfaction. He had done that which he thought impossible. He had succeeded. To-morrow he would drive the horses to Red Bird and hear his decision.

If he said yes, Will would have everything in life he wanted or needed. Red Bird's and Siya-Ka's relatives would provide a tepee and whatever household goods were necessary for a young couple just beginning their married life.

"I have never seen Siya-Ka, but she must be very beautiful," Will's mother said. "May you be as happy as I have been with your father. May your sons grow up to be as fine and brave as my son is."

Her eyes sparkled with unshed tears and Will's throat felt tight. He watched her as she walked towards the house, her body tall and strong, if somewhat thicker and heavier than it once had been.

He climbed to the top pole of the corral and sat looking down at the milling, squealing horses.

Red Bird wouldn't say no. He couldn't. While he wasn't an acquisitive or greedy man, he wouldn't be able to refuse such a gift as this.

He would accept, Will told himself. Criers would go about through the village of Big Foot, announcing Will's betrothal to Siya-Ka, announcing the feast that would precede the marriage.

Then, when that was over, perhaps as soon as three days from now, the tepee they were to share would be erected and furnished. A fire would be built in its centre and all the female relatives of Siya-Ka would prepare a meal.

Siya-Ka would bathe and attire herself in her best deer-skins. Then she and Will would sit together in the tepee, in the sight of all the village, and when they left would be man and wife according to Sioux custom.

Later, perhaps, he would take his bride to one of the black-garbed priests of the white men, and be married according to the white man's law, for he knew this would please his father. But for now, the Sioux ceremony would be enough.

He stared blankly into space, his eyes bright with eagerness. They would eat the delicacies that had been prepared. Siya-Ka's pretty cheeks would be flushed, her eyes downcast from his. The touch of her body against him as they sat together would make his blood race through his veins. The fire would die to embers, and still they would sit.

At last, Siya-Ka would stand and would prepare their bed. She would remove her clothes and would cover herself with blankets. She would wait in the fragrant, smoke-scented darkness.

But she would not wait long, Will thought, for the waiting had already been too long. He would go to her and her lips would be warm and eager on his . . .

He became conscious suddenly that all the light had faded from the sky. Before him the horses milled, biting and kicking and nickering shrilly.

A wind stirred in the north and blew its frosty breath across Will's body. He climbed down from the corral fence and went into the house.

What had seemed impossible four days ago was now possible again. Failure had been turned into success.

Why, then, was his spine so cold? Why was his brain seething with so much unexplained uneasiness? He shook his head impatiently.

Will ate ravenously, then went into his father's room. He found his father much improved. His face again had a healthy colour, though it was still drawn from weakness and pain. Impatience with his own helplessness was beginning to show in his eyes.

Will talked with him for several moments, then headed for his own room, nearly staggering with exhaustion. He collapsed face downward on the bed without even bothering to remove his boots.

His face was covered with a heavy growth of whiskers. His clothes were rank with sweat. Dust and mud were on his boots and clothes. In an instant he was asleep.

But it was neither a restful sleep nor a deep one. He dreamed that he was driving the horses toward the village of Big Foot. As he travelled, a chasm opened in front of him. The horses plunged into it and the chasm closed. Before him, sitting on the back of a spotted horse, was Red Bird. "Where are the horses you were to have brought to me?"

Will could not reply. Red Bird turned his head and called to someone behind him, "Ptesan, I accept your gifts. Siya-Ka will be your wife."

Will tried to spur forward and halt his words, but the chasm opened again and he plunged into it himself. He was falling . . .

He awoke with a cry on his lips. His body was bathed with sweat, though the room was icy cold.

He listened, wondering, filled with a strange sense of unreality. The dream still seemed real, and reality unreal.

He got to his feet and staggered to the window.

His eye caught the movement of something in the yard . . .

The hairs on the back of his neck stirred and seemed to come erect. The thing he had seen in the yard was the dim, skulking figure of a man.

His eyes strained. Then he saw another figure—and another.

Instantly he whirled from the window. He snatched up the Winchester he had intended taking to Red Bird to-morrow. He burst through the door of his room and ran frantically down the hall. From his father's room came the sudden, alarmed question: "Will! What is it?"

"Men in the yard! I don't know who!"

But he did know who. And why. The corralled horses. Nothing else would draw them here. Unless the uprising had begun. Unless the Sioux were going to kill Will and his family and burn their house.

He yanked open the front door, hearing his mother moving about, soothing his father with her calm voice and telling him to lie still. But his father would not lie still. Wounded or no, he would be out the door behind his son before Will had time to find out what was going on. In his hands would be a rifle, loaded, ready . . .

Forgotten would be his wound, though exertion would have opened it and started it bleeding again. Forgotten would be his weakness in the towering anger of the moment.

Will stepped through the door. Already he could see half a dozen silently moving forms. At the edge of the yard he could see their horses, grouped and held by still another man.

His glance went to the corral and a small sigh of relief escaped his lips. The horses still milled within it. If they were after the horses, they didn't have them yet.

A voice shouted something in Sioux, a warning, and immediately afterwards an arrow buzzed past Will's head and buried itself in the wall of the house with a solid, thumping sound. He threw his rifle to his shoulder and snapped a shot at a shadowy form twenty yards away.

The noise of his rifle was like a thunderclap in the otherwise silent yard. Flame blossomed from its muzzle and acrid powder smoke drifted back and filled his eyes and nostrils. A high yell of pain immediately followed his shot.

More arrows thudded into the house behind him. He crouched, and ran, and in an instant broke clear of the house's shadow. He collided with a man and swung at him automatically with his rifle muzzle. The man collapsed in the trampled snow at his feet.

Another gun roared, and another. From the corral came a shrill trumpeting from the horses.

Will ran that way frantically. His blood was heated now and his mind was furious. He knew now who the attackers were. They were Sioux.

They were the ones Will had thought his friends.

And he knew who their leader was. White Buffalo, who wanted Siya-Ka, Ptesan, who knew she favoured Will and had therefore come to spoil Will's chance of having her.

With Will dead and his father and mother dead with him, with their house burned, who would there be to say it had been Ptesan who had done the killing? No one would guess it had been a personal thing. The Sioux nation would be blamed; it would be one more score for the whites to settle in blood.

Will was still twenty yards from the corral when he saw a couple of men struggling to open the gate. And he was faced with the torment of indecision. Should he stop and try to halt them with bullets. Or should he go and prevent the opening of the gate when he reached it—if he reached it in time?

He chose to stop. He flung the rifle to his shoulder and fired. He missed, unable to see either the front or rear sight in the darkness. He fired again.

He heard a cry following his shot, but he was too late to stop the second man. The gate swung wide and the horses thundered through it, trampling the inert body of the man Will had shot.

Too late to stop them. Too late for anything but overpowering fury. The horses were gone and with them disappeared Will's chance of marrying Siya-Ka. Unless . . . unless he could kill White Buffalo and carry his body to Red Bird as proof . . .

Instinct told him to go where they had left their horses, to kill the man who had been left holding them. Then, when White Buffalo returned for his horse . . . Will would have his chance.

He whirled. But he didn't head for the horses as he had planned. He saw a tongue of flame leaping from hay the attackers had piled against the rear wall of the house. He saw his father and mother, backed against the front wall, fighting off three men with clubbed, unloaded rifles.

He ran toward them. There was no time for fighting the fire. There was no time for anything but to join his father and mother and prevent their being killed.

He reached them and fired his rifle blindly at the three attacking them. One man fell. The other two turned toward him.

Will was wild with rage. He saw the knives that gleamed in the hands of the two. He clubbed the rifle and swung its stock in an arc. He felt the impact as it struck one man's head. The sound was like that of an axe biting into a frozen tree. The man went down and the other turned to run.

Will was after him instantly. Ahead, he could see the flurry of activity as the remaining Sioux tried to mount and get away. The man Will was chasing ran like a frightened deer. He wore the soft moccasins of the Sioux and was apparently less exhausted than Will. He began to draw away.

Two or three of the Indians succeeded in mounting, and thundered away. Will wondered if Ptesan was one of them. Or if he was one of those who lay hurt upon the snowy ground of the yard.

A couple of others mounted and galloped their horses away. The man Will was pursuing flung himself to a horse's back. When Will reached the horses remaining there were no men among them. Only four horses, those of the Indians Will had hurt or killed.

Will leaped to the back of one of them. He whirled and headed out in pursuit of the fleeing Sioux.

But he did not go far. His ears had already lost the sounds of retreating hoofbeats. He knew there was no chance either of catching them or of recovering his horses in the dark.

He turned and rode back. By morning, he knew, the horses would be scattered. It would take him a week to gather them again.

The sky above the house was orange from the glare of the flames. A tongue of flame leaped from the peak of the roof.

Already the entire back wall was a sheet of flame. Will's father and mother were hurrying in and out of the house, salvaging a few things they valued. He helped them, and they worked until they were exhausted, until the smoke and heat inside the house became unbearable. Then Will's mother crossed the yard and made a bed of blankets and robes for his father inside the wagon. Will helped him in, and his mother began to remove the blood-soaked bandages from his wound and replace them with fresh ones.

Luke Jordanais's face was pale and wan, but his eyes burned with rage. "When I am well . . . when I am strong enough, I will make them pay!"

"They were led by one called Ptesan who wants Siya-Ka," Will said. "This is my quarrel and I will settle it."

His father stared at him steadily for several moments. Will's face was illuminated by the fire's glare but his father's face was in shadow and he could not see the expression it held.

He helped his mother load the things they had salvaged into the wagon. He went to the barn and got out a team of horses, which he harnessed and hitched to the wagon. Saving a saddle horse for himself, he turned all the others out so that if the barn should catch fire from the house they would not be burned.

He watched as his mother drove the wagon away, toward Pine Ridge Indian Agency. Then he mounted and set out for the village of Big Foot.

He carried the Winchester in his hand. In his belt was his knife. The anger he had felt during the fight, the anger he had known as he looked at the burning house was nothing compared to that which now smouldered in his heart.

Ptesan had taken everything they had: home, belongings. He had tried to take their lives. But there was one thing he would not get, and that was Siya-Ka.

Strangely enough, Will did not blame the Sioux warriors who had helped Ptesan. They had already paid heavily. Besides, Will was sure Ptesan had deceived them as to the reason for the attack. He had probably told them that Will and his father were spies for the whites and were dangerous to the Sioux.

Going to the village of Big Foot was dangerous. Ptesan and his men would have reached the village first and would have filled the ears of the people with lies. Will might never get a chance to fight Ptesan. The Indians might attack and kill him as he entered the village.

Inflamed by injustice and want, stirred up by the Ghost Dance, they might not even listen to him. His jaw hardened. He would have to force them to listen to him. If he did not, and if he failed to kill Ptesan, then he would be forever outcast by the Sioux.

CHAPTER SIX

The distance from Will's burned-out home to the village of Big Foot would take Will several hours to cover. He had gone less than half of it before his weariness began to overcome him. His muscles ached. His head was foggy and felt strangely light. His vision blurred.

He had slept but a short time, he realised, before he had been awakened by his dream. Yet anger kept him awake even though it could not restore his strength which he had used so prodigiously during the past three days. And he would need his strength, all of it, if he was going to defeat White Buffalo.

Will remembered him, though he had never been friendly with him. Ptesan had participated in the Sun Dance at least once, for his left breast bore the scar. Will had heard that while Ptesan was still a boy he had participated in the fight at the Little Big Horn when Yellow Hair and his men were killed. Ptesan had fought several times in war parties against the Crows.

Will must face a skill earned in half a dozen life-or-death encounters. With only anger and determination to help him.

He raised his head and stared at the sky. Unfamiliar with prayers and not sure what God he was praying to, he asked for help.

Then his head sank until it rested on his chest. He slept, and dreamed that he faced Ptesan's knife. Then his ears heard a sound that was like a shout raised from a hundred throats. He jerked awake.

He was chilled and stiff. He looked ahead and saw the winking fires of a village in the distance. He saw the Ghost Dance pole and the dancers. He tried to place the sound he had heard.

Then, while still a quarter mile from the village, he saw that all the people of the village were assembled in one place. They formed a silent throng around a single mounted man.

Perhaps they had really shouted. Will didn't know. Now they were still as death, listening apparently to the man on horseback.

Will drew his horse to a halt and heard the high-pitched wavering notes of a song floating toward him on the still cold air. It was the song of Sitting Bull and, as he listened, he suddenly knew the reason for the crowd's gathering. He knew why the song was being sung. The great Tatanka-yotanka, in whose tepee he had slept, was dead.

He did not realise that his horse had moved on. He was seeing again, in his mind, the calm face of Sitting Bull, the wise old eyes. The manner of the crowd told him instantly how Sitting Bull had died. The soldiers of General Miles had killed him under the pretence of trying to place him under arrest.

The consequences were sure. The Sioux nation would rise. All the villages would unite. Six thousand Sioux warriors would ride against the whites.

The crowd saw Will, and the tone of their voices changed. Then, suddenly, they were utterly silent.

In this silence, the hoarse voice of Ptesan carried clearly to Will. "There is the spy. There is the one who has lived among us only to betray us to the whites. He rode with Goose Face and Red Bird when they went to the lodge of Tatanka-yotanka. He is the one who betrayed Sitting Bull to the enemy!"

Will heard Goose Face's voice rise above that of Ptesan. "Quiet! Let Good Eagle speak! Do the Sioux condemn a man without letting him defend himself?"

The crowd grumbled angrily. Goose Face faced them, never more a chief than he was right now. For, he surely knew, as did Will, that they might turn on him for championing Will.

Will stared into their faces, seeing no friendship, no trust. Their eyes were hard and cold, their mouths thin and cruel. There was savage expectancy in them as though they already saw Will's body, still and mutilated by their knives, upon the frozen ground. A chill ran along his spine.

Only anger could dissipate his fear and uncertainty. And it began to grow in him, the way a grass fire grows before a hot summer wind.

"Ptesan is a liar!" he shouted angrily. "Not only is he a liar, but he is a thief as well and but for luck would be a murderer!"

The murmur of the crowd became like distant thunder. The anticipation in their faces sharpened and Will realised suddenly how much they needed to vent their anger and grief over the death of Sitting Bull.

He raised both his hands and shouted: "I also say that Ptesan is a coward! He is afraid to fight in the clear light of the fires but must skulk through the darkness like a hunting weasel. His boasts of coups are lies! He could not count coup upon any enemy except one that was already dead!"

Ptesan's voice was an incoherent roar. He came bursting through the crowd, intent on pulling Will from his horse and killing him on the spot. Goose Face tripped him and he sprawled to the ground.

When he rose, Goose Face held one of his arms behind his back, a vice grip like iron. Ptesan bellowed: "This is but a boy who knows nothing of courage! This one is white, and one of our enemies! Look at his clothing. It is the clothing of the whites. Look at the hair on his face. Does the Sioux grow hair on his face? I say this one betrayed Sitting Bull to the whites! He is the killer of Sitting Bull as surely as though his own hand held the knife."

Will yanked out his knife and flung it to the ground at Ptesan's feet. It buried itself to the hilt in the frozen ground. "You lie, White Buffalo. You are an eater of flesh. You are a coward and afraid to fight me and so would have your comrades kill me for you!"

His hands and arms were trembling. His face was grey and bloodless. His legs and arms felt like water. But his weariness was gone.

He told himself that he would fight well. If he must die, he would at least inflict a fatal wound on Ptesan before he did. Ptesan would not live to marry Siya-Ka.

"All right, then, let them fight," Goose Face roared. "Let them decide in blood who it is that lies!"

The crowd roared approvingly. They backed away and began to form a huge circle in which three fires burned.

Goose Face looked at Big Foot, who was doubled over with a spasm of coughing. When Big Foot straightened, Goose Face said, "Do you approve of this?"

Big Foot coughed again. When he stopped, his face was shining with sweat. He nodded and choked, "Let them fight."

Will slid off his horse. A boy took the reins and held them. Will handed his rifle to Goose Face and stooped to draw his knife from the ground.

Rising, he searched the ring of faces around him for that of Siya-Ka. He found it, and saw that her eyes were large and tortured, her face pale with fright. But when she caught his eye, she smiled. It was a weak and tremulous smile, but a smile at least.

Her eyes did not conceal her certainty that she was gazing at Will for the last time. Tears shone upon her cheeks.

Will knew he should not have looked at her. He should have guessed how her terror for his safety would show on her face. Love is not brave when it has no hope. And she could have no hope. Ptesan's reputation was too well known, as was Will's youth and inexperience.

He yanked his glance from her and stared at Ptesan, across the circle from him.

He was a large man, not quite so tall as Will, but much more powerfully built. He had the long, hooked nose of the Sioux. Above it, his eyes were close-spaced and narrow. His mouth, though long, was thin and cruel. In his right hand he held his knife and its polished, sharpened blade gleamed like copper in the glare of the fires. He was crouching slightly and his shoulders weaved from side to side as though in some barbaric dance.

Will couldn't take his eyes from the knife. He stared at it as though fascinated.

He knew he had been a fool. He had allowed anger to draw him into a situation from which there was no escape but death. He would have no chance against Ptesan. The fight would be short and at its end he would lie on the ground while his life's blood flowed out . . .

Somewhere in his mind he heard the words "You're goin' to have to fight, so fight like hell when you do."

Fear, which had been like a cold hand resting at the back of his neck, began to leave. He thought of his father and mother, and of their burned-out house. He thought of the horses that Ptesan had scattered. He thought of Siya-Ka in Ptesan's tepee, in Ptesan's arms. And he remembered that Ptesan had lacked courage enough to come and attack Will's home alone.

His eyes sought Siya-Ka again. She was weeping openly, but her face was not contorted. He looked back at Ptesan.

There was too much cruelty in Ptesan's mouth. He would beat her savagely if she failed to please him. There was too much selfishness in his eyes. She would eat only when he had eaten his fill.

Will's anger mounted. It must not happen. He would not allow it to. What advantage Ptesan had in experience, Will would overcome with his youth, with his reason for fighting, with his love for Siya-Ka.

The handle of his knife was cold and hard

against his palm. On silent, wary feet he moved forward toward his enemy.

The blood seemed to drain from his head. Every nerve, every muscle was tightened. They circled as warily as wolves facing each other over a kill.

Their arms were held clear of their bodies. Their legs were bent slightly, ready to spring right or left, forward or back the instant the other moved.

The crowd was silent. The only sounds were those of hoarse breathing and, occasionally, the sound of Big Foot's coughing.

Will was like a man in a rapids now, and knew there was no escape. Yet he had no time for fear. It had disappeared before his intense concentration. Gone also was the weariness in his arms and legs.

Ptesan sprang at him, knife extended, and instantly Will leaped back, losing none of his balance. Before he settled from his backward leap he realised that Ptesan's thrust had been but a feint.

He leaped forward immediately. His knife slashed wickedly and he felt the resistance to its razor-sharp edge as it flicked across the clothing at Ptesan's chest.

Ptesan's shirt opened like a slit grain sack and blood welled from a slash across his chest reaching from breast to breast. Another scar had been added to the Sun Dance scar that Ptesan wore. And a bit of caution had been added to Ptesan's arrogant eyes. No longer were they contemptuous and sure. They became even more intent.

And Will knew something he had not realised before. He was faster than his enemy and lighter on his feet.

Exultation soared through him. There was hope. Ptesan's advantage in weight, strength, and experience might be offset by his own greater speed.

He felt despair evaporate. He heard a laugh, but it was an instant before he realised it had come from his own lips.

Breath sighed from the members of the crowd, as though all had been holding it until the first blood would be drawn. A man's voice taunted, "The claws of the young eagle are sharp, are they not, Ptesan?"

A flush spread across Ptesan's face. His eyes narrowed and this was not a feint. Nor was the attack a slashing one. He drove his knife at Will as though he would bury it in his heart.

His charge was like that of a maddened buffalo. Will had no chance of stopping or turning it aside. His eye caught the copper gleam of the fires upon Ptesan's knife when it was but inches from his chest. He leapt aside, striking Ptesan's knife arm with the heel of his hand as he did.

Then he whirled to face Ptesan again.

The man was slow to turn, for he had been too sure. When he did turn, control and caution were gone from him.

Ptesan charged again, but this time, Will was set and ready. He flung himself to one side, landing nimbly on his feet. He put out a foot and it caught Ptesan's feet and threw him off balance.

He didn't fall at once. Instead he staggered across the cleared circle, trying desperately to keep his feet.

Will could have attacked him from behind. He didn't know why he hesitated. The white man's code, he supposed, learned from his father before he learned the ways of the Sioux.

Too late, Ptesan saw that he would fall into one of the fires. Too late, he tried to turn, to avoid its leaping flames and white-hot coals.

He failed. His hands went out in a last, futile attempt to save himself. Then he fell with his belly and legs across the flames.

His voice ripped from his throat in an agonised scream. He rolled, his clothing smouldering but not afire. He beat at it with his hands.

Had their positions been reversed, Will would have been killed instantly and without mercy. But he only stood and waited until the smouldering embers were extinguished, until Ptesan had recovered his knife.

The man rose and stared at him out of black

and hate-filled eyes. Pain from his burns had maddened him, had stolen what little caution remained in him. He came at Will like something driven before a tornado wind.

Will realised that Ptesan would now make no effort to avoid his knife. He would only try to bury his own in Will, at whatever cost.

Nor would a single death thrust satisfy the burning lust flaming in his eyes. He would literally hack Will's body to pieces if he could. And Siya-Ka would be forced to watch.

Will had no chance to leap aside—only to draw himself up to his full height, to arch his body to one side.

Ptesan's right hand, which held the knife, slid along Will's ribs. The knife edge bit through coat and shirt, through skin and flesh, and scraped the bones. But now the knife was past and while Will was wounded, he was not dead. It was his turn to strike.

He settled back upon the soles of his feet, coming around with all the speed he could command. His knife was like the striking head of a prairie rattlesnake.

Its point encountered the resistance of Ptesan's shirt but it penetrated as easily as a bullet penetrates. It slid between Ptesan's ribs with only the slightest hesitation and buried itself to the hilt.

Leaping away, Will yanked it out and stood

with it in his hand while it dripped blood onto the ground.

Ptesan shook himself like a great, wounded buffalo. He shook his head as though to clear his vision.

Will's weariness returned. Tremors began in his knees and spread until his whole body was trembling. Ptesan took a step toward him as the life gushed from the wound at his side. He took another step and still Will did not move.

He heard a woman scream, and guessed this must have come from Siya-Ka. He heard the voice of Goose Face, "He is dead. Would you stand there and let him carry you to the grave with him?"

But he couldn't move. He could only wait. If Ptesan could reach him, could drive home his knife, it would have to be.

Ptesan could not. From a distance of five feet, Will saw his eyes glaze and grow dull. Ptesan's face, so contorted before, went slack. He pitched forward, his head striking Will's knees as he fell.

Will stood for a moment, looking down. A murmur of approval began in the crowd, as did the resentful cries of those who had been Ptesan's friends.

Siya-Ka ran across the circle, then halted, her eyes downcast. Goose Face and Red Bird stepped to Will's side. "Enough!" Goose Face roared.

"The wrong was against Good Eagle and he has avenged it like a Sioux. It is done!"

"And what of Sitting Bull? What of the betrayal?"

"There was no betrayal. That was but lies from the mouth of the jealous Ptesan. Good Eagle is my brother. He is one of the Sioux. Who attacks him now attacks Goose Face as well."

"And Red Bird!"

"And Stalking Bear!"

"And White Hawk!"

Will saw his friends, those from the village of Goose Face, coming forward now to stand at his side.

He tried to speak, but his throat seemed closed. He took a step toward Siya-Ka.

Suddenly the Sioux, the fires, the village whirled before his eyes. He felt as though he were drowning, as though water was before his eyes through which he could not see.

His head seemed to disengage itself from his body and float through the air like a puff of smoke. Then he saw the stars and was falling, as through endless miles of space.

He struck the ground on his back. He felt the shock of it, felt its hardness and its cold. Then he felt no more.

CHAPTER SEVEN

When Will awakened light was sifting through the smoke hole at the top of the tepee in which he lay. He was covered and warm. There was a tightness about his body, which was naked save for a Sioux breechclout. He groped with his hands and encountered bandages, tightly wound around his ribs.

Looking around, he saw that he was in Goose Face's tepee. Goose Face's two squaws were busy at the other side of the lodge. At the fire, stirring a fragrant stew, was Siya-Ka.

She was kneeling. Her face was intent with concentration. Her back was straight save for the curve just above her hips. Her eyelashes were so long they seemed to lie on her cheeks when she looked downward at the pot.

Will must have stirred, or made some noise, for she looked around at him. Their eyes met unsmilingly and she got up and came to him. She sat down beside him and one of her hands came out almost fearfully and touched his face.

Then she smiled. "Your eyes are clear. You are better?"

He grinned weakly. "I must be. I'm hungry."

"I will bring you some of the stew I have made for you."

She got to her feet. She filled a bowl and brought it to him. Then she helped him up to a sitting position so that he could eat.

Her eyes rested steadily on him as he ate. When he had finished, he said, "I've got to go. Ptesan scattered the horses that were to have been my gift to Red Bird. I've got to gather them up again. Where are my clothes?"

She didn't move. "They were dirty and torn by Ptesan's knife. Besides, they were white man's clothes. I threw them into the fire."

He threw off the blankets and struggled to his feet. His head whirled. Movement opened the wound in his side and he felt the bandage grow warm with blood.

He staggered and would have fallen but for the steadying arms of Siya-Ka. Goose Face's two squaws stared at him unblinkingly from across the lodge. He sat down again. There would be no gathering of horses. Not until his strength returned.

Siya-Ka left the tepee and returned a few moments later with her arms loaded with deerskin clothing. "These are Red Bird's. Wear them. There is no time to think of horses or gifts. The village is preparing to move. The Walks-with-guns are marching towards us. If we are here when they arrive, they will kill us."

She had used the Sioux name for infantry. Hostilities, apparently, had begun. And Will was too weak to fight.

Outside the tepee he heard the crier moving through the village. Afterward he could hear the shouting and noise that accompanies a hasty move.

The men would be going out to catch horses. The women and children would be gathering household goods and packing them in rawhide bags.

He finished putting on the clothes Siya-Ka had brought him. He realised that while he had been unconscious someone had washed him. Siya-Ka said, "Lean on me. We must go to Red Bird's lodge."

Will's head seemed to float as he walked. The air was cold and he began to shiver violently. He supposed he had lost a great deal of blood and that probably explained his weakness.

The first tepee came down. The hide covering was rolled up, tied, and placed on a travois. Then came the poles, one by one. Lastly the three main poles came down, the ones that supported the weight of the lodge.

In an hour there would be nothing left of the village. Nothing but the discarded toys of the children, their sleds made from the rib bones of cattle or buffalo, their mud and grass horses and men, their make-believe villages. Nothing but the blackened remains of fires and the circular marks left on the ground by the tepees.

The village would move faster than the infantry.

"Where are we going?" Will asked.

"Into the badlands. Or perhaps just outside of it."

They reached Red Bird's lodge. It was already partly down. Red Bird was working at it, helped by the wives of his friends.

Weakness had almost overcome Will. When Siya-Ka released him, he nearly fell. She helped him to a seat upon a pile of rolled-up buffalo robes, then left him and began to help with the work.

Will closed his eyes. He could see only futility in running, for there was no place they could be safe. They could go into the badlands, of course, where the soldiers would be afraid to follow. And yet, how long could the Sioux live there? There would be no food except for that which they could carry with them or steal by night forays against the ranches outside. Ammunition would run low from their skirmishes with the troops. And the winter's bitter cold would settle in.

Wood would run short. The people would grow weak. In the end surrender to the whites was inevitable.

Will could see that none of his own misgivings were shared by the Sioux. Most of them were excited. The excitement of the young men showed in their sparkling eyes and eager faces.

The older ones may have suspected that defeat

was inevitable and only a matter of time. Yet even to these, death apparently seemed preferable to starvation and slavery.

The children were frightened, for this was something new in their experience. The women concealed their feelings behind masks of wooden expressionlessness that almost seemed to be indifferent.

Will knew it was not indifference. They were vitally concerned. But they did not question the wisdom of their men.

Preparations were completed at last and the village moved away. No orders were shouted. No one was told where his place in the caravan would be. Each took a place silently and each did that which was required of him without urging, without orders.

The contrast between this and the way of the whites brought a wry smile to Will's pale lips. He imagined the confusion that would ensue if the whites tried to move a village of four hundred in an hour's time.

Red Bird helped Will to the back of a horse. Then he rode away to help with the horse herd. Siya-Ka rode at Will's side, glancing fearfully at him as though trying to guess his strength and his ability to last out the trip.

Will clung determinedly to his horse's mane with both hands. He didn't want to ride a travois like a sick old man or a squaw.

Nothing had been said about Ptesan and he knew nothing would ever be said. It was done . . . finished . . . Ptesan was dead.

Will suddenly had a bleak feeling of despair. He knew a chilling certainty that he would never live to marry Siya-Ka. He was wounded and weak. Mending would take days, even weeks perhaps.

By the time he was able to ride, there would be nothing to ride for. His father's horses would be stolen or hopelessly scattered. His cattle would have been eaten by the Sioux. There would be nothing to give Red Bird.

Besides, an Indian war was going on, and it would not be over soon. It would last until the Sioux were starved into submission. Or until they had all been killed.

Yet in spite of his despair, there was a new peace of mind in Will. He was, at least, with the Sioux. He was one of them. He had bought his right to be one of them with blood.

No longer must he live in a half-world as his father and mother did. He belonged. And it was worth whatever must be its cost.

Siya-Ka, beside him, seemed like a sister or a nurse. To-day she did. But that would change. When his strength came back . . .

Horses or no, gifts or no, war or no, she would be his wife, he told himself. A Sioux marriage where gifts were neither given nor received was not unheard of. There were times when a man and woman simply ran away together and they were not penalised for doing so. They were considered married as surely as though custom had been adhered to.

He stared straight ahead and clung fiercely to the back of his horse. His jaws clenched themselves determinedly.

The day dragged endlessly. It became to Will a struggle during which he fought unconsciousness with every bit of his strength.

Off to one side of the moving village travelled the horse herd, several hundred strong. Some of the young braves acted as horse herders. Others, in small parties, scouted ahead, on both sides and to the rear of the moving village.

The Walks-with-guns, they reported, were fifteen miles to the rear, and moving fast. They were slowly closing the distance between.

At midday, the village halted briefly and the women prepared food. Siya-Ka brought Will a bowl of stew, but he was too weak to eat. She spooned it into his mouth as though he had been a child.

He was ashamed to eat this way, but he couldn't help himself. It was all he could do to hold his head erect and swallow the food.

But he felt stronger afterward. And he climbed stubbornly onto his horse's back.

He could see, if the Sioux could not, what the

future held in store for the Indian race. Perhaps, he thought, this was the last time that half a thousand Indians would move across the plain this way.

The old things would go until the Indian would no longer be recognised as such. Feathered war bonnets would be replaced by the white man's felt hats. Long braids would disappear in favour of hair cut short. Deerskin clothing would be unknown.

The Sioux would lose themselves in the white race. This would be the dying struggle of the Sioux, and they would die proudly. They had seen the change though their hearts had never accepted it. They had seen the plain when it lay empty and untouched for a thousand miles and more. They had seen the herds of buffalo blackening its reaches for as far as the eye could see.

They had known the secret of living from the land alone. They had known how to catch and tame the wild horses, how to utilise to its fullest extent the bounty of the buffalo. They knew how to capture the eagle, how to kill the cougar when he hunted too close to their villages.

Night came and they camped, though the lodges were not set up. They camped, and built fires and ate, and afterward slept rolled in blankets and buffalo robes.

Will slept as though he were dead. He knew

nothing until he heard the criers calling, "Co-ooo-o," which meant "Get up."

The village stirred. Fires were freshened and rebuilt. Meat was cooked. Patrols came in and fresh ones went out. The returned patrol members squatted on their heels and related the numbers of the pursuing infantry and their location.

The white men's feet were sore, it was said, and they were suffering from the cold. They were discouraged, too, feeling that they pursued a company of ghosts which they could never catch.

They were right, thought Will. They would not catch the Sioux, who could lose themselves in the untracked wilderness of the badlands.

Siya-Ka came to Will and bathed his face. She combed his hair with gentle fingers. Will scraped the whiskers from his face with his knife, which Siya-Ka had washed and whetted until it was like a razor. He ate, and afterward felt new strength flowing through him.

He mounted carefully, so that he would not reopen the wound. He rode away with the moving village. Siya-Ka travelled by his side again. To-day her lips smiled often and her eyes were bright.

She had been terrified, he realised, that he would die. Now her relief at seeing him improved was so great that at times she seemed almost hysterical.

Will felt a wave of tenderness toward her. And,

combined with it, came an uneasy feeling of fear. The future held danger for her. Somehow he must protect her from it. Her body must never lie white and cold upon the snowy ground.

He looked at her, and reached for her hand. It was small and cold, yet it had the strength of her own fear in it. She clung to him, as one drowning would cling to a rescuer and her eyes, brimming with unshed tears, looked desperately into his.

Her voice was small. "What is the end to be, Good Eagle? Will my body die barren, without having known your son? Will we all die, like cattle, under the guns of the Wasicun?"

Will knew that she needed him now as she never had before. He said hoarsely, "You will live to teach our daughters to be good wives and I will live to teach our sons to be brave and strong. Some of the Sioux may die, but never we two. It cannot be."

His words seemed to comfort her, for she released his hand after a final squeeze and gave him a timid smile. And the day wore slowly past.

That night they camped again, and again, before daylight, were on the move. Will's strength seemed to be increasing more rapidly now and he did not tire to-day until the sun had set behind the hills.

His wound was beginning to itch, which Siya-Ka said was a good sign. She also told him that his face had regained some colour.

No longer were her eyes tortured with worry. Instead she smiled often, and sometimes laughed. To Will's ears the sound was as beautiful as that of a mountain stream in early spring.

Often that night her hands reached out to touch him, as though she wanted to reassure herself. And with much of his weakness gone, her touch stirred Will as it never had before.

Morning came, and again the crier woke the villagers. Again they moved on. In midmorning a patrol came racing to them to announce that the Walks-with-guns had turned back. A cry of triumph went up from the people as though this were a victory and not but a brief respite.

Perhaps only Will knew how hollow was the victory. Perhaps only Will realised how tenacious the whites could be. He knew their overwhelming numbers. He knew their nagging fear of the war-like Sioux.

This winter war would not last long. But for a little time the men of the Sioux nation could live in rebellion like men. A week. Perhaps even a month. Then it would end. In starvation and defeat. In death for some.

He, himself, must live a lifetime, if possible, in the few short days ahead. For those days would be as the old days had been, filled with the excitement of the hunt, the chase, the comradeship of other men who faced the same mortal danger. They would be rich with fulfilment.

And he would be a man, wholly a man, before he died. He would plant his son in Siya-Ka.

As for the Sioux, was it not better, he thought, for them to live as free, brave men and die so than to live as cattle domesticated by the whites, even if the time for living so was short?

He glanced aside at Siya-Ka. He smiled. The smooth skin of her face grew pink. Her eyes looked into his, as naked of subterfuge as his own.

She would come to him to-night. When the lodges were up, when the night was a robe of softness across the world, then would she come and share his bed.

Soft and warm and proud, she would lie in his arms and in the morning they would face the people of the village and say, "We are one."

They camped, in late afternoon, on the bank of the Porcupine. Big Foot and his sub-chiefs had decided that living here would be easier than in the badlands. There was plenty of water and grass for their horses. If danger threatened, they could move swiftly into the trackless depths of the badlands. Also, from here, raiding would be easier and food more plentiful.

But there was another reason Big Foot did not move into the badlands. Already thousands of the Sioux were there, bands more powerful than Big Foot's band, with chiefs of more authority.

Had they gone in, Big Foot would have been

forced to accept that authority and his band's identity would have been lost in the greater numbers of those already there. He would lose his right to think and act independently and to an Indian that right is most important.

Perhaps, thought Will, the very independence of the Indian was why the whites had so consistently been able to defeat them. For the tribes had never been able to unite.

Had they been able to do so, Cheyenne, Arapaho, Commanche, Apache and Sioux could have put forty thousand warriors into battle. The whites would have been held back for twenty years.

While Will rested, Goose Face's tepee went up, and Red Bird's next to it. Goose Face and Red Bird came riding in from duty with the horse herd, and grinned down at Will when they saw him looking so well.

There was a twinkle in Goose Face's eyes. Smiling mockingly, he turned to Red Bird and said, "I am taking a party out at nightfall to steal some beef. I want you with me."

He glanced at Siya-Ka, busily working on the tepee and she caught his glance and flushed with embarrassment. Will met his glance, but he could not help feeling confused. Goose Face laughed, but it was not an unkind laugh. He knew Will's love for Siya-Ka. He also knew that time might well be short.

Red Bird scowled, but his scowl sprang more from a feeling of duty than displeasure.

Siya-Ka disappeared into the tepee with an armload of firewood. Because Will could no longer stand sitting still, he got up and walked away to search for more. It was not a man's job, this wood-gathering. But Siya-Ka had enough to do and no one to help her.

Besides, the activity would calm Will's thinking, calm the mounting excitement that grew stronger in him as the light in the sky grew faint.

He had healed swiftly because he was young. If he moved carefully and did not twist a certain way, his wound gave him little trouble. If he did not reopen it again . . .

Perhaps to-morrow he could ride with the others, if not on a raid, then at least to hunt. He was anxious to be useful and a part of things.

Try as he would, he could not keep his thoughts from straying back to Siya-Ka. In his mind he saw her, small and finely shaped. He saw the curve of her back, the exciting glimpse of brown thigh exposed by a quick, unthinking movement. He saw her eyes, saw their eagerness and the quick, shy smile of her lips. His hands, gathering firewood, trembled.

Suddenly he could no longer stand being away from her. He hurried through the village to Red Bird's tepee and burst inside, to drop the firewood he had gathered just inside the flap.

She was kneeling beside the fire, which was burning brightly. Smoke rose from it toward the hole at the peak. It billowed out, reaching it, and made a cloud in the upper third of the lodge.

"Red Bird will be absent to-night," Will said.

Her voice was very small. "Siya-Ka shall not miss him to-night."

"Nor will I."

He wanted to touch her, to lift her up, but he did not. Instead he sat down cross-legged on a buffalo robe and watched her work.

Her hands, though small, were deft and quick. Her eyes were downcast and again it seemed to Will that her long, black lashes rested upon her flushed cheeks. Occasionally she would steal a glance at him and when she did would moisten her lips with the tip of her tongue and smile with shaken nervousness.

At last the meal was ready. She gave him his bowl and would have watched while he ate. But Will had been raised as a white and he said, "Sit and eat with me."

It seemed to please her. She sat down timidly beside him and began to eat.

They ate swiftly, nervously and without speaking. Afterward they sat, strangely still, and in expectant silence watched while the fire died to glowing embers.

Outside the lodge, the village noises gradually quieted, even to the barking of the dogs. The people of Big Foot's village were weary to-night and sought their beds early.

Had it not been for the exhaustion of their three-day trek, Will knew they would have heard the singsong chant of the Hanpape-cunpi players as they gambled far into the night. They would have heard the lutes of the village lovers as they played and waited before the tepees of their desired ones. They would have heard children crying and perhaps the quarrelling, somewhere, of a brave and his squaw. But not to-night.

When the village was completely quiet, Will got to his feet. He did not look directly at Siya-Ka. Standing beside his bed of robes and blankets, he removed his deerskin clothing. Then he got under the blankets and waited, watching the shadowy form of Siya-Ka beside the dying fire.

He was as tense as the sinew string of a bow. Nerves jumped in his arms and legs. Siya-Ka rose.

She moved into the darkness beyond the fire. He heard the rustle of her garments. Then he felt her beside him, slipping beneath the robes as he had done.

He turned and put his arms around her. She was trembling as though she were cold, or afraid. He felt her cheek with his own and found it wet with tears.

He drew her close to him gently, controlling his

desperate urgency in a wave of tenderness. And while he held her, her trembling ceased.

Will's voice was hoarse as he murmured softly into her ear, "I will always love you, Siya-Ka. You are . . ."

She did not let him finish. Her soft hand was upon his mouth, silencing him, and he knew that her fear was gone.

The trembling and the weeping were done, and so was the speaking. They became as one, blending together in the darkness, and even in their young awkwardness there was beauty.

They were like children, beholding their first snow, transfixed by its beauty. They were the old ones, whose eyes gaze with awe into the promised land of Wakan Tanka. They were the warriors, fasting upon the mountain top, whose eyes may see glories denied all others.

All these they were, and more. Then they lay in peace, clasped tightly in each other's arms, and slept.

When Will awakened, Siya-Ka had left their bed. She had built up the fire and was making coffee and frying meat. She looked at him, a teasing smile touching her mouth.

Will threw off his blankets and stood up. There was only a slight twinge of pain in his side. He stretched cautiously and laughed suddenly for no reason except that he felt like it.

He put on his clothes. Siya-Ka watched him steadily, her eyes holding an expression that made him feel strong and warm inside.

He was a king, a chief of the Sioux. He was the richest of men, for he had Siya-Ka.

She would bear his son and the boy would grow brave and strong and tall. She . . .

Red Bird entered the tepee. He saw their faces and scowled. Will faced him and said, "The waiting was too long and the time too short. Siya-Ka and I are one."

For an instant there was anger in Red Bird's face. His eyes turned hard and his mouth was a thin line in his dark face. Suddenly and unexpectedly, then, he smiled. "I will go and tell the village."

He turned and left the lodge. After a while, Will heard a crier moving through the village announcing a feast and announcing their marriage.

It would take three or four days for the relatives and friends of Siya-Ka to make a tepee and furnish it with necessities. When that had been done and when everything was ready, there would be a feast, just as though all the customs had been adhered to.

Yet Will knew that three days was a long, long time. Much could happen in three days. It was possible that they would never occupy their lodge.

If they did not, at least they had known the joy of possessing and of being possessed. They had known one night together even if it was to be all they ever had.

CHAPTER EIGHT

The day was one of settling the village securely in its place beside the Porcupine. Lodges, hastily erected the night before, were now made secure and tight. Travois, left untouched in the previous night's rush, were now unpacked and their loads stored away.

A hunting party came in with several deer. A raiding party came in with a dozen head of cattle. For the rest of the day the village air was rich with the smell of cooking meat.

Will could almost imagine that this was as it had been in the old days. He could almost forget the whites that surrounded them.

He could imagine that, by riding out, the men could view the endless herds of buffalo that dotted the plain, that their only enemies were those of their own kind who sometimes trespassed upon their hunting grounds.

The warriors of the village sat before their tepees in the thin sunlight, cleaning their guns, making arrows or sharpening knives. They knew fighting would come. Yet they showed no fear.

All of a Sioux warrior's training points to the day when he will die in battle. Fathers exhort their sons to bravery, to death if it be the alternative to caution. Will's father had put it more like a white man would in saying, "Fight like hell when you fight," but the meaning had been the same.

Older men came in with a great, tall pole which they had cut in the woods nearby. It was forty feet long, and they dug a hole in the centre of the village and set it there, upright.

It fluttered with scraps of bright-coloured cloth. Even before it was securely set in the ground, some of the men began a Ghost Dance around it. Women joined them each wearing a white feather in her hair.

Will would not dance because he did not believe in it, nor was he expected to because of his wound. So he and Siya-Ka walked out together into the hills. Hand in hand they walked, like children.

They ate the wasna she had brought along. They lay side by side in a protected hollow where the sun gathered its warmth. They leaped from rock to rock, crossing the icy streams, and laughed when they slipped and wet their feet.

They walked for miles, as far as the badlands' rim, and they looked down into its fastnesses and marvelled at how it came to be.

Will saw a buck deer, grey as steel, his neck swelled with the mating season. He saw two bull elk, battling on a high pinnacle. He saw a bear, shambling through the woods, pawing aside old stumps in his search for grubs. The jay and the squirrel scolded, and Will and Siya-Ka laughed at them.

In late afternoon, when the sunlight was orange upon the trees, they made themselves a bed of dry leaves, and loved again, and afterward dreamed of the son that would be theirs.

Home to the village in early, smoky dusk. Home to the cries of the Ghost Dancers, to the silent, stolid onlookers who seemed as frozen statues sitting in a ring around the pole.

Home. And it seemed to Will as though he had never seen the inside of a white man's house, as though he had not worn white men's clothing and spoken the white man's tongue.

His father, his mother, his early life all seemed like a dream, of no real substance, of only vague memory. This was now his life.

Siya-Ka prepared their night meal. Red Bird and Will ate together seated beside the tepee's fire. Afterward they sat before the tepee, and smoked, and watched the children playing as though the peril of the Sioux did not exist.

A dozen yards away was a small play-tepee, in which three small girls were playing at being grown. Farther on, several boys were playing Can-wa-ki-ya-pi, or tops, and the tops made a humming noise as they spun. Still others rode stick horses into battle and made *bang—bang* noises to represent guns. Some of these shot arrows at a white bone placed in the crotch of a tree.

There had been no opportunity before for Will to ask about the death of Sitting Bull, and he did so now. Red Bird's mouth thinned with anger as he answered.

"It was planned to kill him, not to take him alive. Indian police went into his camp first and the Walks-with-guns stayed nearby in case of trouble. Bull Head led the police and they surrounded Sitting Bull's lodge. They called to him to come out. Sitting Bull was alone in the tepee with his two sons. One of them cried out and when he did, Bull Head and the police rushed in. They shot Sitting Bull and both his sons, one of whom was only twelve years old."

There was disgust in Red Bird's voice as he went on. "Bull Head, whom Sitting Bull had wounded, took his scalp. Another of the Indian police, in a frenzy, beat Sitting Bull's head and face to a pulp with a plank. They looted his tepee, taking even his clothes as souvenirs. One of the people of Sitting Bull's village brought the story to our village. He said that on Sitting Bull's body was a letter from a white woman named Weldon in New York City warning him to flee as the government was about to have him murdered."

He was silent for a time, and Will waited. At last Red Bird said angrily: "They did not even allow his relatives to honour his remains by placing them in the crotch of a tree and shooting his favourite horse nearby so that he would not have to walk to the land of the Wakan Tanka. Instead they are taking his body to one of their laboratories where they will cut it into little pieces to see what made him great. But they will not find the spirit of Sitting Bull in his remains. It lives in the heart of every Sioux."

Will asked: "What will Big Foot do if the whites come after us?"

"He will fight. If they come with war, we will give them war."

They talked of war and of other things, and the hour grew late. At last they rose and went into the lodge.

Siya-Ka was already in bed. Red Bird grinned at Will as he slipped into his own bed on the far side of the lodge.

Will went to Siya-Ka, filled with the peace of belonging wholly at last. The future might hold misery and death. But the present held only Siya-Ka.

Will was awakened a couple of hours before dawn by Red Bird, shaking his arm. "Come quickly, Good Eagle. A train of wagons has been found, not a dozen miles from here. They are carrying food and guns and ammunition for the guns. We are going to capture them."

Siya-Ka had awakened too, but Will said, "Stay and sleep. I will soon be back."

"Sleep while you are gone and in danger?"

Will touched his cheek to hers. She did not try to hold him or to make him stay. Instead she got up and watched him while he dressed.

He finished, snatched up his rifle, and followed Red Bird out into the bitterly cold, frosty morning air.

Hoarfrost lay heavily on the ghostly arms of the trees and turned the weathered, smoky tepee coverings to silver. It lay also upon the ground and squeaked beneath their moccasins.

A boy came running with their horses. They mounted and thundered after the others leaving the village ahead of them.

Nervousness touched Will as he rode. But it was the nervousness of excitement. Guns and ammunition would be tremendously valuable to Big Foot's band. The food would be equally valuable.

In the cold, Will's wounded side, though it was healing well, began to itch and burn. His hand, holding the steel receiver of the Winchester, grew numb with cold.

Forty strong they rode, pushing their horses hard. Goose Face led the party and he rode with the two scouts who had discovered the wagon train. From them he ascertained the road upon which the train was travelling, its speed and direction, so that he could point his men along an intercepting course.

The sky grew faintly grey in the east. In its

ghostly light, Will glanced around at the galloping war party.

Tall men all, they rode straight and relaxed upon the bare backs of their horses. The faces of some still wore the blue paint of the Ghost Dance. Others wore one, or two, or three eagle feathers in their hair. Some of their horses were painted for war, and in their manes and tails were tied bunches of eagle feathers. The men were armed with rifles, lances, and bows.

Most notable were their expressions which were intent, savage, and filled with anticipation. Too long had the Sioux been beggars, waiting beside the corral at Pine Ridge for their inadequate rations of food. Too long had they listened to the cautious words of the old ones.

Now, again, they would ride like men, taking that which they needed from their enemies, the whites. Once again they would bring honour to the tribe.

The grey spread from the eastern horizon until it covered the entire sky. The thin cloud mass that lay in the sky turned pink, then orange, and at last the sun poked its brassy roundness above the rim of the world. Before it had risen high, they reached the road the wagons had been travelling.

Goose Face had apparently planned well. Will saw no fresh wheel tracks on the road. The wagon train had not yet reached this point.

Goose Face gave his orders quickly. Swiftly

they moved back from the road, concealing themselves behind rocks and trees, their horses at their sides.

And they waited, in utter silence, their only movement that of their chests, rising and falling with their breathing.

They did not have long to wait. In the distance they heard the faint shouts of the teamsters, the squeaking of a dry axle, the dim rattle of harness and tugs. Then the wagons came into sight over a slight rise half a mile away.

The train was strongly guarded. Four Longknives rode ahead and four behind. One was an officer and he wore at his side the long sabre from which the name Mila Hanska, or Longknife, derived.

Scarcely breathing, the Sioux waited. Will's eyes gleamed with anticipation and his hands trembled with eagerness. There were eight wagons in the line, each drawn by two teams of mules.

A cry came from Goose Face and Will vaulted to the back of his horse. The Sioux swept down upon the train from both sides, yelling and shrieking and firing their guns.

A cavalryman fell from his horse and lay still. Another slid off when the animal reared. He got up and ran towards one of the wagons but fell as a bullet struck him and he lay twitching on the ground.

Panic ripped through the cavalry guard, for the first to fall had been their officer and now they were leaderless. Like quail, disturbed by a running horse, they scattered and fled, until they were lost to sight over a long, low hill.

One of the teamsters was bent over, hugging his belly. One of the Sioux was down, his dead eyes staring sightlessly at the sky.

The mules halted and the wagon train was still. The remaining drivers were now down beneath their wagons, firing with calm hopelessness. The Sioux were too many for them and they knew they had no chance.

Circling and firing, yelling like demons, the Indians rode around the stalled wagons. One by one the teamsters died until at last the battle noise was stilled, the guns silent.

Will and his comrades gathered around the wagons and ripped away their canvas covers. With rifle butts they smashed boxes of food, rifles, and ammunition.

Then they tore the canvas covers into squares, each brave took a square and filled it with food and ammunition. Carrying this and as many rifles as he could, he would awkwardly mount his horse.

Will followed suit, but because of his wound, could not manage the burden and also mount his horse. Red Bird handed up the sack and rifles to him.

Much had been left behind, but much had been taken. And neither rifles nor ammunition had been overlooked.

No one considered the possibility, apparently, that the dead they left behind would be identified, or that the village of Big Foot would be singled out for vengeance and retribution.

But the dead would be recognised, and cavalry would descend on the village. It was only a matter of time.

Their victory and the loot they had captured caused great elation in the village upon their return. Quickly the rifles were distributed and hidden. Quickly the provisions were concealed. Half an hour after their arrival, nothing was visible that would have pointed to them as the guilty ones.

The proof was hidden. And now, too late, it occurred to Will that their dead would be identified as soon as the wagon train was found. Furthermore, forty men, heavily loaded, would leave a trail it would be impossible to miss. Unless it snowed and Will doubted if it would.

He mentioned his misgivings to Red Bird, who brushed them impatiently aside. Red Bird didn't care if the whites did know they had been responsible for the raid. He would welcome an attack upon them by the whites.

Will realised the others would also welcome it.

They neither expected nor wanted to avoid the coming clash.

Then why, he wondered, had they taken such pains to hide the loot? To satisfy the old ones and women, he supposed, who did not realise that such a plain trail had been left behind.

He calculated the miles that lay between the wagon train and Pine Ridge Indian Agency. An eight-hour ride for cavalry. The surviving members of the guard would reach it in that length of time or less. Allow another four hours for preparations and another eight for the avenging cavalry to reach Big Foot's village. To-morrow afternoon or night then, he thought.

He went to sleep thinking that, to-morrow, he would ride out on scout. He would ride far in the direction of Pine Ridge, so that he would be able to return and give ample warning of the cavalry's approach.

He awoke in early dawn, to the harsh, startled cries of the village guards. In no more than his breechclout, Will ran outside, clutching his rifle in his hand.

He stared around him in dismay. Surrounding the village were the blue coats of the mounted Longknives, hundreds of them. Their voice shouted orders in English, in Sioux. "Surrender! Surrender or die!"

The village had no choice. The U.S. Cavalry had come upon them during the night. The guards had no doubt felt secure, as Will had, in knowing the cavalry could not possibly reach them from Pine Ridge before late that day. What they had not counted on was the possibility that troops were approaching even as they attacked the wagon train.

Surrender was their only salvation. Surrender dictated by force. But none in the village of Big Foot felt despair. The troops could not confine a whole village, even if they managed to drive them back to Pine Ridge. The braves could escape. Perhaps the whole village could move again.

In guttural Sioux, the word passed through the village. "Show no resistance. This is but for a little while. They will have to leave us and go after another band and then we can escape again. Only next time we will go into the badlands where we will be safe."

Under the supervision of the cavalry troops, the village came down and was loaded again onto travois. Once more they began to travel, this time toward the Indian Agency instead of away from it.

For a while, Will rode with his friends. Then he realised that he might be useful if he rode within earshot of the whites. He could listen to their talk and report the things they said to Big Foot and the other chiefs.

Goose Face and Big Foot were glad to have him

do so, and he gathered much useful information. For one thing, he learned that the cavalry officers had not expected to capture the band, that they had been surprised to find them outside the badlands.

He discovered that they believed capture of Big Foot's band would calm the terror infecting whites all over the Dakotas. He also learned that other white commanders had moved in their troops to strategically seal the escape routes from the badlands.

Not that the Sioux wanted to escape, he thought. When they were ready, they would come out, and come out fighting, convinced that they were doomed anyway, that the white men wanted to exterminate them.

In Big Foot's moving village, the talk was of nothing but escape. And war. Capture seemed to have changed the minds of those who had still counselled patience. All the men of the village travelled with their weapons beneath their blankets and robes or within easy reach hidden in travois loads. They slept at night with them by their sides.

Three long days passed. At last, on the third night, the village of Big Foot reached the place the cavalry wished them to camp. They put up their lodges hastily so that they could be quickly taken down.

That night few of the cavalrymen slept. And all

night Will stayed awake, listening to their talk. His knowledge of English was tremendously valuable now. He had not been recognised and they didn't know everything they said was overheard.

He learned that General Nelson A. Miles had set up headquarters at Rapid City with some one hundred and fifty soldiers. General Eugene A. Carr was at the junction of the Rapid and Cheyenne rivers with four hundred more, ready to move on Pine Ridge immediately. Seven companies of the 17th Infantry had been sent from Fort Russell to Pine Ridge to reinforce those already there.

A party of fifteen Sioux had tried to fire a ranch on Spring Creek. Carr had sent a hundred men to the rescue. He overheard them talking about the wagon train Goose Face had attacked and of the "valiant" fight put up by the cavalry escort.

Will passed on each bit of information he heard to the chiefs. Three times, runners slipped from Big Foot's village to carry messages to those in the badlands and advise them of developments.

Thus it went for two days. On 20th December, General John R. Brooke sent a force of five hundred so-called "friendly" Indians into the badlands to try and persuade those inside to surrender. On that day, the cavalry guarding Big Foot's village was withdrawn.

No sooner had they disappeared from sight than

the villagers began to move. Swiftly the tepees came down, to be loaded again upon the travois.

And no sooner had they begun to move than it began to snow. Wind howled down out of the north. Snow whipped along horizontal to the ground.

Siya-Ka clung to Will like a shadow. There was a haunted look in her dark eyes as though she had been given sight into the future and saw terrifying things.

Will rode with the wind beating into his face and she rode at his heels, her eyes ever on him. If he turned, he met her gaze. If he dismounted, she was there beside him.

Children rode muffled in blankets and robes, either on horseback or if they were small on travois. Babies rode on their mothers' backs in the traditional Hoksicala Postan, the Indian cradle. Their faces were not exposed and all Will could see of them was the lump they made beneath their mother's blankets.

He wondered how the whites would like this war they seemed so determined to force upon the Sioux if they were forced to make war hampered by their homes, their possessions, their women and children. How would they like fleeing across the icy plain in the teeth of a howling blizzard?

Would they close their eyes to the wan, drawn look of silent weariness upon their loved wives' faces?

Will didn't suppose they would. Their hearts would hurt as the Sioux hearts hurt because they could do nothing to stop cold and weariness and fear. They would weep inside as the Sioux now wept.

The storm continued, its fury unabated. All day they travelled, pausing but briefly in the afternoon to eat. Small fires were built and over these huddled the chilled and suffering people. They thawed frozen chunks of meat over the fires on sticks and ate them partly raw. And then went on.

Not much new snow had fallen, less than three inches in all, Will guessed. But the wind kept blowing it along the ground, filling the air with it, collecting it in hollows and ravines.

Will took his turn at riding scout, and was relieved, and rode scout again. Always when he came back to Siya-Ka, he would feel her eyes on him even before he picked her out from the anonymity of the blanket-wrapped throng.

Little more of her than her eyes was visible. She rode, hunched with cold, on the back of a stocky paint horse. Blankets covered her head and swathed her body. Even her hands were hidden in the blanket's folds. But she did not complain. Few of the people did complain. They were free again.

The daylight hours slipped away. Night came down, bringing no slackening of the wind, which made an eerie, whistling sound as it struck the resistance of their bodies.

Near midnight they camped, and again small fires were built. And upon the snowy ground they went to sleep, exhausted and thoroughly chilled.

Siya-Ka clung to Will as though she feared this might be their last night together. And Will held her very close until utter weariness claimed his mind.

They moved on before dawn streaked the sky. Mercifully, the wind had stopped blowing sometime during the night. But the air had grown more bitterly cold than before.

There could be no glory in fighting under such conditions. There could be only suffering, both for the Sioux and for the whites. A wounded man would freeze where he lay in a few short hours' time. Blood would freeze as it dripped slowly from a wound.

But it was the condition of the children that tormented him the most. Their whimpering and crying was a low, continuous sound throughout the village. Mothers tried to warm their children by holding them close against their own bodies, but they could not hold them long for it was impossible to travel thus.

A child of seven died of the cold and of the cough it brought on. A woman, blanket-wrapped and riding a travois, bore a child but the child never uttered a cry. It died before she could clasp it in her arms.

And Big Foot was desperately ill. Many times Will would hear his rasping, choking cough. Goose Face told Will the chief's face was red and blotched with fever. Will saw him once through the driven snow and his shaking was so violent it was visible through his blankets.

Hopelessness and despair walked through the moving village. They would never reach the badlands. They would freeze before they did. The badlands were too far away.

But in afternoon of the second day, Goose Face and Will rode ahead, slipped past the cavalry guard and into the badlands under cover of the storm. Immediately, though their supplies were short, those already there began preparing food for Big Foot's band. And Will and Goose Face returned to guide the village in.

Goose Face gathered together a force of fifty men. They rode ahead of the village until they encountered the cavalry guard. Howling and firing their guns, they encircled the white cavalry and forced them to fort up behind the protection of their supply wagons. When they had done so, they rode a circle around them until the village had passed and entered the badlands beyond.

The village was safe, Will thought. The children would grow warm again, the women rested. All the people would once again eat hot food.

Of the future, Will refused to think. He knew, if the others did not, that the cavalry guards on the badlands would increase in numbers until at last they outnumbered the Sioux inside. Those troopers under Major Whiteside, part of the Seventh Cavalry, had been pinned down easily. But how easily could they be engaged when their numbers were twenty times what they were right now?

The Seventh Cavalry. Will's mouth twisted wryly. Custer's outfit, whose esprit de corps still demanded vengeance for the fight at the Little Big Horn.

He refused to think of the future because he knew it held only death. For himself, certainly. Perhaps even for Siya-Ka.

CHAPTER NINE

The badlands, useless for any ordinary purpose, served the Sioux well as a refuge now. A hundred miles long and forty miles wide, it was a wonderland of strange formations caused by ages of wind and water erosion.

Will had heard it said that the badlands was once a huge lake, and supposed it could be true for he had, himself, found impressions of fishes and shelled creatures in its rocks.

Many times he had sat his horse on its rim, staring out across it, looking down where it dropped away beneath his feet, a maze of oddly shaped, bare hills, of narrow, twisting canyons in which no streams ran.

Though he felt convinced that the Sioux were doomed, he still tried to convince himself that it was not so. He told himself that many a doomed cause has triumphed because of the determination of those who believed in it. He asked himself if this could not now happen with the Sioux.

They put up their lodges, sheltered by the canyon walls from the icy bite of the wind. They ate of the hot food prepared by their friends already here. They rested, and slept far into the following day.

Now the people of Big Foot's village began to

enter into the activities of the gathered Sioux. Some danced the Ghost Dance. Others rode out on raids. The women went about their domestic tasks.

In the night, in the silence and warmth of their own tepee, Will and Siya-Ka clung to each other with a passion born of the fear they shared. How long, Will wondered, before his seed could take root in Siya-Ka. It must be soon, he knew, for there was not much time. They lived only for each other now, knowing each night might be their last, knowing each morning might see their last farewell.

The white man's Christmas came and went, uncelebrated among the Sioux except that many of them exclaimed contemptuously at the white man's hypocrisy. And it was not long after this holiday that a new enemy came among the Sioux. An enemy they could not fight. An enemy they could not see. The enemy was disunity.

The old ones began to talk surrender. The young shouted a fierce refusal.

Nor was this the only source of disunity. There was no one chief to lead them all.

Sitting Bull could have led them, Will thought. But Sitting Bull was dead.

So they bickered endlessly around the council fires. One favoured luring small detachments of cavalry inside the badlands and slaughtering them. Another thought they must go out in force and sack the white men's towns. Another thought they should send runners to the northern Sioux and persuade them to join in a general uprising.

Big Foot attended the parleys, though he was too weak to walk and had to be carried there. So did Goose Face. Will himself often stood at the rim of firelight and listened to the talk.

But it was only talk. And often he wandered away, discouraged and disturbed.

Perhaps Big Foot's patience was short because of his illness. Whatever the cause, he spoke out angrily two days after the white man's Christmas in the council of the chiefs. He told them he was disgusted with them and disappointed because they could not agree. He said that henceforth he alone would make the decisions for his band.

The council broke into angry shouting during which many made threats of reprisal against all who went out and surrendered to the whites. Big Foot laughed at them. He shouted, "Then show me a chief who will lead us all. Only then will I stay and fight."

A young man in the crowd drew a knife, his face ugly with anger. Will quickly drew his own knife and stepped between the man and Big Foot. The young man may have witnessed his duel with Ptesan, for he sheathed his knife and turned aside.

Big Foot's sons carried the chief away. Goose Face followed and was followed in turn by

Red Bird and Will. Reluctantly and unwillingly came the young men of Big Foot's village, not agreeing, but bound by the word of their chief.

There were four hundred in the village of Big Foot, of which a hundred and fifty were warriors. It was not a decisive force, Will realised. Not large enough to force an issue or decide a point. Yet perhaps large enough to set an example for the others.

Will went to his tepee, newly made and furnished for he and Siya-Ka by her relatives and friends.

Her face welcomed him. A fire was burning brightly in the centre of the lodge. An iron pot steamed and bubbled on the fire and the air was rich with the warm odours of cooking meat.

She brought him a pair of moccasins she had made for him, decorated in the old way with dyed quills instead of beads. Her eyes were shy and her expression begged for his approval.

He examined the moccasins, feeling the soft texture of the leather, noting the meticulous stitching, the exquisite quill work. "They are fit for a chief to wear," he said approvingly.

Her face glowed. She flung herself into his arms and threw her arms around his neck. He discovered that she was trembling and her words were a cry. "Good Eagle, I am afraid! What is going to happen?"

Will shook his head worriedly. "Big Foot has

walked out of the council," he said. "To-night or to-morrow he will decide the course our village will take. Perhaps we shall go out and meet the whites alone. Or perhaps we will surrender. But I have a feeling that the end is near."

His words should have added to her fright, he thought, even though that had not been his purpose in speaking them. He had simply felt she was entitled to know what was going on.

But they did not add to her fright. They seemed instead to calm her. She drew away and looked into his face with eyes that seemed to devour it. Her voice was small but steady. "Then to-night must not be spent in trembling or in fear. It must be lived, as though it would surely be our last."

Will's throat felt as though it had closed. His eyes burned. Her smile was forced, but it was a smile. "Sit by the fire. Our meal is ready."

Will sat cross-legged on the robes that covered the floor. Siya-Ka brought him a steaming plate of meat. He motioned for her to sit and eat with him.

It pleased her, as it always did. And as they ate, she chattered of all the things she would make for him during the long winter months. She talked of the clothing she would make for their son, not yet conceived. "He will look like you," she said as though that would be the most wonderful thing that could happen to him.

Intruding faintly into the tepee from outside were the yells of the Ghost Dancers, the wrangling around the council fire. Will could not help thinking that perhaps Big Foot was the wisest of all the chiefs. By going out, by facing the whites alone, Big Foot's village might bring unity to those who remained behind.

Would he surrender, or would he fight? Will couldn't guess. If he elected to fight, what would happen to Siya-Ka? Big Foot had indicated that he meant to take the entire village out.

White soldiers were not always particular whether they killed a man or a squaw. Will had heard it said jokingly that any blanket-wrapped Indian looked the same in a rifle's sights. He knew as well how many women in the village of Black Kettle had been killed at Sand Creek years ago.

He looked at his wife, and touched her, and drew her close to him. They sat together, warm and alone, until the fire died and the village noises quieted. Then, in the chilling dark, they sought their bed.

It was wrong, Will thought, that their love should die when it had lived so short a time. It was wrong that death could intrude so soon upon their lives.

As the tepee fire had died, so at last did the fires in their bodies also die. They slept peacefully in each other's arms.

• • •

In Will's first waking moment he knew what Big Foot's decision had been. Criers were waking the village. There was no call for the warriors to assemble. Big Foot meant to surrender his band.

Siya-Ka woke with a start and stared at Will with dazed and frightened eyes, but nothing was said between them now. They had said it all the night before. They had lived the night as lovers do and were content.

Will arose quickly and dressed. Siya-Ka began to rebuild the fire. Her expression was strangely stolid and fatalistic, a quality Will had not seen in her before.

They ate hastily and then Will went out to catch horses and rig a travois. When he returned she had the tepee down and ready to be loaded.

Only one travois was needed, for they had not yet accumulated much in the way of household goods. Will loaded it and helped Siya-Ka lash their possessions down.

There was confusion among the other villages as the people watched Big Foot's band preparing to depart. Young men rode at top speed through the village shouting taunts. Squaws from the other villages screeched insults at the squaws of Big Foot's village. Even the children fought.

A delegation of chiefs came to confer with Big Foot, but left soon afterwards, shaking their heads. And at last all was ready for the move.

Without command, almost as though by common consent the village moved away toward the edges of the badlands. Will waved to Siya-Ka, then rode out to join the other warriors who would ride ahead. No guards were needed, either at sides or rear. Whatever danger they faced to-day was straight ahead.

After the blizzard of several days past, this day was a relief. The sun shone warmly down. A south wind blew its gentle breath across the land. The sky was cloudless and as blue as the turquoise ornaments of the Navajo.

Big Foot was so weak he could scarcely sit the back of his horse. Goose Face, his favourite among the sub-chiefs, rode beside him, alert to catch him if he should start to fall.

He should have ridden a travois, thought Will, where blankets could have warmed his fever-ridden body and stopped the violent shivering that shook him from head to foot.

His face was like carven stone, as implacable as the great rock towers of the Black Hills. But it was red from fever and his lips were almost blue. Often he went into spasms of coughing. When he would stop his face would be running with sweat.

Will wondered if Big Foot realised how close to death he was. Did he really mean to surrender them, or was he leading them out to fight so that he would have company on the long journey to the land of Wakan Tanka? Will shook his head.

Slowly the hours passed. The sun climbed across the sky, and warmed the land and thawed the snow. The ground turned soft and muddy under the hoofs of their horses. Water ran in dry ravines and dripped from rocks that lay on all sides of them.

Nervousness increased in Will. His hands and knees trembled. For he knew that even though Big Foot meant to surrender, he might not be given the chance. The whites were ugly and afraid. They might attack the instant the band emerged from the badlands, might give Big Foot no chance to tell them he wanted to surrender.

Out of the badlands they rode, knowing their chief's intent but proud and straight and strong upon their horses. Plumes and feathers fluttered in the wind. Savage faces, smeared with war paint and with the blue paint of the Ghost Dance, showed bitter disappointment and a belief that they were more than equal to the white man's cavalry.

They came out of the badlands, and saw no enemy. So they went on, descending at last into the valley of the Porcupine where they had been captured before. To the rear of the warriors came the village, more slowly moving but no more than a few short miles behind.

They rode down a gently sloping, grassy plain,

and saw on the far side of it the blue uniforms of the Longknife cavalry.

Will knew he would never forget the scene. The air was clear and sharp, like the water of a tumbling mountain stream in early summer. There was a faint smell of wood-smoke hanging over the valley. The earth beneath his feet drank eagerly of the melting snow.

The sound of jangling accoutrements came clearly to Will's ears though the distance between Indians and cavalry was over six hundred yards. Big Foot raised a hand and his warriors halted in their tracks.

Now sounds were muted as their horses fidgeted. He could hear the harshly indrawn and exhaled breath of the braves on either side of him.

Their faces were drawn, their eyes narrowed. Their feathers stirred in the soft south wind. Will could feel the baffled anger in them. They did not want to surrender. They wanted to fight.

Only then did Will realise that Big Foot's decision had not yet been made. For the chief raised a hand, signalling his men to array themselves in a battle line.

They did so instantly, their eyes shining fiercely once more. Straight as an arrow the battle line stretched across the thawing ground. A step ahead of it Big Foot sat his horse, swaying from weakness.

He would be first to fall, Will thought. He might even fall from weakness before he had even been hit.

He stared across the valley toward the cavalry. And suddenly the dream he'd had in the village of Sitting Bull came back to him.

This was the valley he had seen in the dream. Across there where the whites had also begun to form a battle line were light cannon and Gatling guns. Big Foot's warriors would not get past the centre of the valley. They would be slaughtered before they even got close enough to fight.

If Big Foot elected to fight, as it now seemed he might, his men would be cut to bits. Will glanced down the line at the faces of his friends.

In each he saw the same certainty of defeat he felt himself. They knew they could not fight cannon and Gatling guns. Yet in none did he see fear or the desire to retreat.

Across the clearing now, Will heard the voices of the whites. Then a single man rode out, alone.

Will strained his eyes, but could not recognise him. He rode slowly and deliberately until he reached a point midway between the Sioux and the cavalry. Then he stopped.

Big Foot turned his horse and looked down the line at his men. His face was ghastly. Sweat stood out in beads on his forehead. But his eyes were fierce and they shone with pride.

Having satisfied himself that his warriors

were ready, that they would accept his decision, whatever it might be, he turned and rode toward the white man who sat his horse alone out on the plain.

Big Foot's hands clung to the mane of his horse. His body swayed with weakness. But as he approached the white man, his back straightened and his head came up. The plumes and feathers of his war bonnet fluttered.

Apparently the white cavalry officer could speak no Sioux, and Big Foot certainly knew no English. After a few moments of unsuccessful talk in sign language, Big Foot turned his head and stared back toward his men.

Will heard his name called and turned his head. "Ride out, Good Eagle, and interpret for him," Goose Face said.

Will touched his heels against his horse's sides and galloped toward the pair. Immediately a trooper began to advance from the white men's side.

Will reached the chief and drew in his horse on his left side and a little behind. Big Foot, without turning, said, "Tell him that Big Foot is tired of running and now will fight. Tell him that many of the Longknives will die."

Will repeated the words in English. The officer listened but did not speak.

Big Foot went on: "Tell him the Sioux only wish to live in peace. They are friends of the whites. But their children are hungry and their lodges cold. The Great Father sent them cattle and told them to raise more. Then he reduced their beef rations so that they had to eat the cows which were to have produced calves. Tell the officer of the Mila Hanska we would like to live in peace but we would rather die fighting than by starvation."

Will interpreted, wondering where all this was leading. Still the white officer remained silent. His face was cold and growing colder. Will thought that if the cavalry had not outnumbered the Sioux, he would have been more receptive.

Big Foot continued for several minutes more along the same line. At last his voice dwindled and he sat silently, breathing hard.

Only then did the white officer speak. His voice was like a whip. "I have heard this talk before, and I have only one answer for it. Surrender. Surrender at once or we'll blow you to bits!"

Will interpreted for Big Foot and saw his face turn cold. The chief stirred and reined his horse aside as though to go back to his men.

The officer spoke again, this time hastily, his voice less cold, his words less clipped and harsh. "It may be that the Great White Father has made a mistake. But he relied on those who counted the Sioux. Surrender and there will be another count. There will be more beef for the Sioux, more blankets, and land for each man, young or old."

Will could have shouted with triumph. For all the Indians' smaller numbers, the whites were afraid of them. Else they'd have made no concessions at all.

He was tempted, briefly, to misinterpret the officer's words. Yet he knew the responsibility of decision was not his. So he interpreted exactly as the officer had spoken.

Big Foot's shoulders relaxed. Even before he spoke, Will knew what his words would be.

Big Foot would surrender his village. Will wanted to interrupt, to tell him that the officer's words were lies. He had no authority to speak for the government, to make promises to the Sioux.

Besides that, and the officer surely was aware of it, a fight here might be a temporary victory for the U.S. Cavalry because they outnumbered the warriors of Big Foot's band. But less than a dozen miles away, inside the badlands, were enough Sioux braves to slaughter this officer's whole command. And they surely would, when they heard the gunfire, come out and join the fray.

Big Foot spoke almost reluctantly. "I believe your words. I surrender." He looked at Will to interpret for him.

Will wanted to shout, "Don't you know he's lying? He can't speak for the government. His promises are as empty as all the others have been!"

But he didn't speak. Big Foot was dying, as surely as though a bullet had penetrated his heart. His eyes held a pitiful, forlorn hope. He believed the officer only because he desperately wanted to believe.

Will saw, in that instant, a glimpse of the awful weight which responsibility places upon a leader's shoulders. Big Foot had carefully weighed the lives of his men against the good their dying might cause. He had found their lives more valuable. He had made his decision and Will could not question it.

He turned. In sign language he indicated that Big Foot had surrendered them.

They sat their horses as though stunned. Angry words flew back and forth along the line. Then Will heard Goose Face shouting angrily at them. Their shouting stopped.

"Tell them to rejoin the village," the white officer said. "We will then surround it with guards and lead the way to Wounded Knee Creek where they are to camp. Tell them no one will be hurt or punished."

Will rode back to the line and repeated the words of the white officer to Goose Face, loud enough so that the men could hear.

Their faces were scowling. There was puzzled, angry frustration in their eyes. They had prepared themselves to fight and die and the order to surrender was like a blow.

Nothing had been said about their weapons, Will realised. Nothing would be said, he supposed, until they reached the camp on Wounded Knee Creek and the whites were reinforced.

Big Foot came riding back, clinging with desperation to his horse's mane, swaying drunkenly on the steed. Behind him came the cavalry, riding slowly. When they were two hundred yards away they stopped and waited nervously.

It was a touchy moment. A moment when a spark could have fired the spirits of the Sioux, when they might have refused the edict of their chiefs and fought in spite of it.

Goose Face's eyes were cold and stern. He waved an imperious arm toward the rear where the moving village was. A warrior turned reluctantly, then another warrior. Then, suddenly, they were all turning and riding with slumped shoulders toward the rear. Will could guess their feelings from his own. He felt humiliated and degraded.

They reached the village with the cavalry a quarter mile behind. The whites were both wary and fearful, aware that the Indians still had their arms. But with things as they were, the whites were afraid to insist that they be disarmed.

Will and the others joined the moving village. The cavalry split to let it pass through their ranks. Then they formed on the village flanks and rode along pacing it, carbines resting on their knees.

They need not fear now, Will thought. Not an Indian would start anything, knowing that a single shot would bring about a savage massacre of women and children.

Big Foot fell from his horse before they had gone a quarter mile. He was picked up and placed on a travois where he was wrapped warmly with blankets. He looked like a lump of clay riding there, without life or spirit.

Will held his fidgeting horse still, allowing the village to move on past. His eyes searched anxiously for Siya-Ka.

He saw her at last, near the rear of the village. Her eyes were also searching and when they met Will's lighted in a way that made him forget the humiliation of the surrender. He rode to her, dismounted and walked with her.

He would not have been human if he had not been glad that they could be together, that they could live in peace once more.

In peace? Then why the uneasiness that lived in the back of his mind? He glanced to the side of the column and studied the faces of the white soldiers riding there. He read the legend on the fluttering guidons.

And then he knew. Their captors belonged to the Seventh Cavalry, the outfit that still smarted under the unavenged defeat of Custer at the Little Big Horn on 25th June, 1876, fourteen years before.

Big Foot's village had surrendered but it was not safe. It would not be safe until the Seventh had been relieved from guarding them. Or until the wounded esprit de corps of the Seventh had been avenged.

CHAPTER TEN

All through the day they travelled, with the troopers of the Seventh close upon their flanks.

As their gloominess increased, so did the spirits of the cavalrymen increase. With returned confidence, they shouted back and forth to each other jubilantly as though they had won a victory in battle, as though they had defeated the Sioux. Will understood their words and was glad his comrades could not. He refused to interpret for his friends, or even for Siya-Ka.

The Sioux warriors rode sullenly, angrily. Will realised that they knew they had been surrendered for nothing but a few empty promises.

The sun dropped in the western sky and the air grew cold. The thawed and muddy ground began to freeze and harden beneath their feet.

Siya-Ka rode beside Will, glancing worriedly sometimes at his face. Once she said, "I am glad there will be peace as all our women must be glad. My heart was torn when you left me this morning for I knew I might not see you again except to mourn and bury you. It was hard for me because our time together had been so short.

"Now, perhaps, we can be together always. We will raise many strong sons to carry on the Sioux battle against the whites."

Will's uneasiness returned but he did not mention it or tell her things were not settled yet.

Dusk crept coldly across the face of the land. Night came down, and in early dark they reached Wounded Knee Creek where the whites shouted at them to halt.

Fires were built and food was cooked. They ate, and then the tepees were raised. Travois were unloaded and their loads carried inside. The horse herd went out into the grass, herded by a dozen young men.

On a nearby hill winked the fires of the cavalry guard. And all through the night riders galloped in and out of their camp, challenged each time by the sentries, carrying, Will supposed, messages to and from Pine Ridge.

Other sentries were stationed around the village, spaced less than a hundred yards apart. These also filled the night with their cries, giving the numbers of their posts and the information that all was well.

As often as not, Will would be able to detect fright in their cries, for all that they tried to sound unconcerned. And he realised that these men, like those in the Indian camp, were young and untried and full of doubt.

He tossed restlessly in his sleep and several times awakened Siya-Ka with his dreaming. Once he dreamed that the village was surrounded by cavalry. General George Armstrong Custer himself, yellow hair waving, stood on a hill and shouted, "Fire!" and bullets and grape shot cut through the village like a scythe through grain. He awoke, sweating, the cries of the dying Sioux ringing in his ears. Siya-Ka calmed him with her cool hands stroking his sweating face.

What did the future hold for them, he wondered as he stared upward at the few stars visible through the smoke hole at the tepee top. What lay ahead for them? Will's lot had been cast with the Sioux and his fate would be the same as theirs. But would they be allowed to remain in the Dakotas now? Or would they be shipped away on trains as other tribes had been?

He had no answers for the questions that tormented him. But he did have Siya-Ka and she comforted him in the only way she knew and at last he dropped off into a deep and dreamless sleep.

When he awoke, the first deep grey of dawn lightened the smoke hole at the tepee's peak. For a moment he lay still, listening and remembering.

Usually, when Will awoke, he was relaxed, but this morning he was not. Every muscle in his body seemed tense, every nerve drawn tight.

He turned and awakened Siya-Ka. She smiled sleepily before opening her eyes and then her arms reached out for him.

Feeling his stiffness, she opened her eyes and

looked at him. Immediately she sat up, concern written in her face. "What is it, Good Eagle? What is wrong?"

He shook his head. "Nothing, I suppose. I just feel . . . Oh I don't know."

She smiled again. "It is the restless night you spent. You slept little and dreamed much. Lie still. I will fix you something to eat."

She got up and dressed quickly. But from her paleness Will knew his uneasiness had been communicated to her.

He heard the calling back and forth of the guards outside the village. He heard the barking of the dogs, who would not accept the soldiers' presence as silently as their masters would. He heard the fitful crying of a child, the shrill scolding of a squaw.

These were the normal village sounds, yet to-day they were muted because of the presence of white men in the vicinity of the camp.

Will got up suddenly and dressed. He went out, walked to the stream, stripped and plunged into the icy water. He did not linger, for the water made his body turn blue and made his teeth chatter audibly. He ran all the way back to the lodge, carrying his clothes.

He sat down to eat as soon as he had dressed, relieved to discover that the icy bath had relaxed his body completely although the odd, depressed feeling of unease still lingered in his mind.

"They will try to disarm us to-day," he said. "They will have sent for reinforcements and when they arrive, will take our guns."

"Will the men give them up?"

He shrugged. "Most of them will. But there may be a few . . ."

"Talk to Goose Face about it. He will know what must be done to make sure there is no trouble."

He nodded. Her advice was good. By himself he could do nothing to make sure the disarming would be peaceful. But with Goose Face's help . . .

He got up and left the lodge. He went to Goose Face's tepee and entered. "Is Big Foot better?" he asked.

Goose Face shook his head. "To-day—to-morrow—soon he will die."

"The Longknives will want our guns to-day," Will said.

Goose Face shrugged. "What must happen will happen. Perhaps all the men will give them up peacefully. But we are not soldiers, who blindly obey whatever orders are given them."

Outside Will heard the soldiers shouting. Goose Face and he went out and watched a column of reinforcements arriving. "Go to a place where you can hear their talk," Goose Face said. "Listen well and when you return tell me what they have said."

Will wandered near a group of soldiers. He

dared not get close enough to hear every word for he knew he might be recognised as Big Foot's interpreter.

He heard a name, "Colonel Forsythe," and some garbled talk that to-day they'd show the damned redskins a thing or two. He heard one man say ". . . get their guns and then we'll have them where we want them."

They were not reassuring utterances. Repeated verbatim, they might serve to further convince the Sioux that they were to be disarmed and killed.

He returned and repeated what he had heard to Goose Face, who stared at him solemnly and asked, "What do you think, Good Eagle? You have lived among them and know how they think and what is in their hearts. What will they do to us?"

Will frowned. "They are under the command of their officers and will do as they are told. Most of their officers are good and responsible men who must answer for what they do to their superior. I think if we give up our arms we will not be hurt. But I also think that if one shot is fired . . . I think anything could happen then. This is the Seventh Cavalry, which was defeated by the Sioux at the Little Big Horn. Yellow Hair is their hero and they would like to avenge him and erase his defeat."

Goose Face nodded, but he did not speak. If

Big Foot died, he would be chief. If Big Foot was unable to rise and speak for his people, then Goose Face must speak for them.

They were roused by a shouting among the white men who surrounded the camp. Goose Face got up and Will followed him out.

There was an officer before Big Foot's tepee, accompanied by about a dozen soldiers. All were dressed in round fur caps with the ear flaps tied up atop the caps. The officer wore a long greatcoat and had black, shiny boots, the tops of which reached beyond the hem of the coat.

Goose Face strode to the officer with great dignity and stopped. "Tell him I will speak for the chief."

Will repeated Goose Face's words in English. The officer said, "I am Colonel Forsythe. I have your camp surrounded. There is a Hotchkiss gun trained on you and several Gatling guns. You will order your warriors to assemble."

Will repeated his words to Goose Face. A number of warriors had gathered curiously. Goose Face issued a few crisp orders to them and afterward they dispersed, some of them scowling fiercely at the officer and his men.

Will's uneasiness increased. He watched the face of the white soldiers closely.

Forsythe maintained an almost stoic calm, which Will suspected was not altogether genuine. The soldiers looked either frightened or defiant.

From all sides the Sioux warriors began to assemble. Most of them were wrapped in blankets against the cold. Squaws and children came from their tepees and then concealed themselves behind the tepees. Their faces could be seen peeping fearfully from the places of concealment.

Will glanced toward the high ground beyond the camp. There, soldiers were drawn up in a line, rifles held at ready. There were groups around the Hotchkiss gun and Gatling guns.

He had told Goose Face he thought it would be safe for the Sioux to surrender their guns. Now he was not sure. He wished he could call back the words, but he knew he would not even if he could. This was their only chance. Even with weapons the Sioux were no match for the cavalry surrounding them. And to fight from the village . . . to draw such murderous fire while their women and children were here . . .

The warriors were now assembled, in a sullen, defiant group. The officer looked at Will. "Is this all?"

Will nodded. "It is all."

"Tell them to send out a group of twenty."

Will told Goose Face what he had said. Goose Face called out twenty names. Twenty warriors stepped forward. They moved out away from Goose Face's tepee to a cleared space about fifty yards away. Immediately they were surrounded by soldiers, carrying their rifles at ready.

It had been orderly so far, Will thought. But how long would it remain orderly? One insult, one slight, and tempers would flare out of control.

Will hurried to the place where the twenty warriors stood and spoke to the soldiers in English. "Tell me what you want of them and I will tell them in Sioux." A red-faced sergeant spoke. "We want their guns, mister. Just tell them to give 'em up."

Will translated. The warriors looked puzzled and stood shaking their heads. Will spoke quietly to the sergeant lest their shaking heads be interpreted as refusal. "They have no weapons as you can see. Their guns are in their lodges."

The sergeant hesitated. He walked over and conferred with Colonel Forsythe. Afterward he came back, his face even redder than before with an anger Will did not understand. "All right," the sergeant bellowed, "tell 'em to go get their guns. Bows and arrows too, an' lances, knives an' tomahawks."

Will repeated his instructions in Sioux. The twenty turned and disappeared among the lodges of the village.

Will waited anxiously. His body felt cold and there was an empty feeling in his stomach. If the twenty did not return, if they opened fire on the soldiers instead from places of concealment . . .

Apparently the soldiers were thinking the same thing. They kept turning their heads uneasily.

Their hands were white upon the stocks of their rifles.

The sigh of relief that came as the twenty began to reappear was plainly audible to Will.

But not all of the twenty carried guns. Will saw only two. These were tossed onto the ground before the soldiers. Beside them were dropped two or three old tomahawks and a single lance.

It was hard for Will to keep from smiling despite the tension of the moment. His amusement disappeared when he glanced at Forsythe's face. It was pallid with fury. The man's lips were compressed and his eyes blazed.

"All right, damn it!" the sergeant barked. "If they won't bring 'em out, then we'll go get the damn' things!"

He issued a few crisp orders to his men. About forty of them began to move through the village, searching first one tepee and then the next.

Will saw the outraged fury in the faces of the hundred and fifty assembled warriors. He prayed soundlessly that they could hold their tempers, that they could swallow the insult inherent in the violation of their homes. If they could not . . . if one squaw screamed . . . then all of them, their women and children too, would die here upon the frozen ground.

For several moments silence, or near silence, hung over the scene. The searching parties of soldiers went quietly through the village. The only sounds were those of the jangling weapons they collected and occasional short commands issued by their noncommissioned officers.

Among the group of stunned and outraged Sioux, anger began to grow. Muttering back and forth swelled from a murmur to a low rumble.

Alarm traced itself upon the faces of the officers. Colonel Forsythe bellowed an order and the dismounted cavalrymen began to close in, their rifles at ready, muzzles pointed toward the Sioux. They closed until they were only twenty feet away, then stopped.

Their expressions more than their nearness convinced the warriors they intended to fire. The looks on the soldiers' faces ranged from abject terror to fierce anticipation and sadistic delight.

A warrior began the death chant in a voice so low Will could scarcely hear it. But it was taken up by others, one by one, until it became a mournful dirge that reached to the farthest corners of the camp. And, for the first time, doubt showed in the face of Colonel Forsythe.

He had played his hand, and now knew he had over-played it. He commanded a part of the Seventh Cavalry, over five hundred strong. His regiment had a grievance against the Sioux.

Will watched him closely. He seemed to hold his breath and slowly the anger ebbed from his face to be replaced by a kind of quiet desperation.

Retreat was out of the question. He had allowed this to become a matter of pride, and face, both for his own men and for the Sioux. Yet if he went on with it, and his expression plainly showed his conviction about this, he was courting disaster.

The death chant continued, its minor key adding to Will's uneasiness. The tension mounted steadily.

How long, Will wondered, would the death chant last? Would it end with some warrior leaping into the air, screaming a war cry, and hurling a tomahawk or knife into the close-packed ranks of the whites?

But the chant died and the Sioux waited silently. The soldiers who had searched the camp returned and dumped nearly a hundred rifles on the ground. With them were countless less deadly weapons, bows, arrows, lances, knives, and tomahawks.

Forsythe's colour returned. With it returned his composure and his arrogant superiority. He knew he had the upper hand again. He had the weapons of the Sioux and no longer feared their toothless snarls.

"All right!" the Colonel shouted. "Now search their damn' lousy bodies, one by one!"

Will stepped toward him swiftly. If a single soldier laid a hand upon a Sioux before the warrior understood his intent . . .

He shouted in Sioux, "They wish to search your

bodies now. They do not believe they have all the weapons and think some are concealed beneath your blankets."

Forsythe yelled at him, "Tell 'em to line up. We'll go down the line and search!"

Will felt a traitor as he repeated his instructions. He felt ashamed, as though the order were his own.

Hopelessness, defeat, shame, and humiliation showed in the faces of the warriors as they formed a line. No longer were they the proud race who had met the whites in a hundred battles, who had beaten them and thrown them back . . .

The line moved forward until two-thirds of the warriors had been searched. Yet Will's uneasiness persisted. Only a few knives had been found and one tomahawk. Nothing else.

Relief was apparent among the whites. It showed plainly in the faces of both Colonel Forsythe and Major Whiteside, standing with him now. Will glanced back at the sullen line of braves. . . .

He saw the bulge of a rifle beneath the blanket of the brave next in line. He saw it, and opened his mouth to shout.

Too late. The warrior leaped out of the line, snatching the rifle from beneath his blanket. He levelled it, his eyes completely wild . . .

Will recognised him, though he did not know him by name. The man was known throughout the village as being not right in his mind. Now . . . unless . . .

The rifle's roar was like thunder in the silence. One of the cavalrymen cried out, and stumbled forward to fall face downward almost at Forsythe's feet.

Forsythe bellowed something at his men, but his voice was lost in the spiteful bark of a score of rifles.

Goose Face clutched his belly and folded quietly to the ground. The line of warriors which had been searched was torn apart. A dozen men fell, leaving great gaps in the line. On the ground the wounded writhed, their cries audible above the continuing crackle of carbine fire.

Growing panicky, the cavalrymen began to retreat, firing as they went. Will stood as though frozen and not until the Gatling guns began to chatter did he move. He ran to Goose Face and knelt . . .

The chief was dead. Will glanced up, stunned.

Half a dozen of the Sioux warriors had snatched knives and tomahawks from the pile on the ground and had charged the line of retreating cavalrymen. Rifles crackled and the six went down . . .

The Sioux had yet to strike an effective blow, save for the single shot fired by the simple-minded one. Yet nearly a dozen cavalrymen lay dead or dying on the ground.

It was an instant before Will understood why. Then he realised that their own comrades, who had the village surrounded, had killed them by excited and indiscriminate firing.

Will didn't seem able to move. He was not afraid, though he knew death was only seconds away. Only when he saw a child, a tiny girl of five, try to run from camp and be cut down did he spring into action. He leaped for the pile of weapons on the ground.

He reached them and seized a rifle. It was empty so he flung it down and seized an iron-headed tomahawk and knife. The little girl lay in a crumpled heap.

In that instant something happened to Will's mind. An instant before he had been too shocked, too unbelieving to move. Now, knife in one hand, tomahawk in the other, he charged toward the kneeling, calmly firing line of troopers fifty yards away. As he did one cavalryman leaped to his feet with a hoarse yell, "Remember Custer!"

Will's tomahawk split his skull. A bullet caught at his sleeve, another, intended for him, thudded into the cavalryman's body. Already dead, the trooper collapsed at Will's feet.

Will turned, his sanity returning, and ran like a deer in the direction of the village. A bullet grazed the side of his head, bringing a sudden rush of blood. Then he was sheltered by the tepees and, for the moment, safe.

Passing Big Foot's tepee, he saw the riddled body of the chief lying twisted on the ground in front of it. Blood welled from a dozen holes in the naked upper half of his body. His face was like wax, and his eyes were open, staring sightlessly at the sky.

The shouts beyond the village continued as the cavalrymen rallied to their battle cries "Remember Custer!" and "Remember the Little Big Horn."

All around Will was death. Dogs died, bullet riddled. Children, babies in cradles on their mothers' backs. Young women. Boys.

Will lost all control of himself. He was wild with rage. He wanted to kill, and kill again, to slash and tear with his bare hands. Bullets cut through the tepees around him, fired blindly, killing impersonally.

Women and children ran toward the rear of the village, but even in retreat there was no hope. The village was completely surrounded by the whites.

Into Will's mind came a name, that calmed his lust to kill, that filled him with a terror new to him. Siya-Ka! Was she one of those who lay upon the frozen, snowy ground? Or was she one who crawled in pitiful torment, dragging shattered limbs in the snow and leaving a wide, red trail of blood? Did she yet live?

Finding escape cut off at the rear of the village,

the people ran in terror to the front again. They began to mill in helpless confusion, sheltered from the view of the whites by the tepees, but not from their rifles' fire. Will knew that somehow a way must be opened through the whites so that they could escape.

He stared around him helplessly. He saw Red Bird standing alone before his tepee, arms folded, waiting for death to strike. "Red Bird!" Will yelled, and ran toward him. "Where is Siya-Ka?"

Red Bird pointed wordlessly. Will stared in that direction but could not see her. She was gone. She was dead.

The noise was terrible. Everywhere the screams of the women and children, of the dying, were a continuous sound. Above it rose the disordered crackling of rifles, the wicked spitting of the Gatling guns. Occasionally the cannon would bellow and grape shot would cut through the tepees like hailstones.

Will shook Red Bird violently. "We've got to do something! We've got to try to open a way so that people can escape!"

Red Bird stared at him for a moment without comprehension. Then understanding touched his face. He shouted, gathering to him every able-bodied warrior within hearing.

They seized rocks, clubs, whatever came to their hands. Twenty strong, they moved to the rear of the village where the line of whites was thin.

Behind them came the women, those without children, those who were young and strong and unhurt. Their hands also held whatever weapons they had been able to find.

Reaching the edge of the village, they crawled through the high grass beyond on their bellies. When it no longer would conceal them, they rose and charged, screaming like madmen.

A soldier crumpled under the club in Will's hands. Before he was still, Will seized his rifle and levered a cartridge into the chamber. He fired at another trooper and saw him go down. Clubbing the rifle, he smashed another aside.

The skirmish was over in minutes, and an escape route was opened for those still able to flee. Fortunately, those Red Bird and Will had attacked were in a small draw and their deaths went unnoticed by the troopers on either side.

Survivors streamed up the draw and disappeared over the ridge behind. Women and children. The old ones, frightened and confused. Boys and girls, weeping uncontrollably.

Will watched each face as it passed. He helped all those he could. He knew that Siya-Ka was dead or she would have passed through here with the others.

At last those who could travel were gone. Remaining were only the dead, the crippled, and those few of them who now would fight.

Will looked down into the village. From this distance there was something impersonal about the bodies which lay like scattered dolls upon the snowy ground. There was something unreal about the few that moved, trying to crawl yet knowing not their destination.

Behind him, he heard a renewed firing. Red Bird stared at Will, his eyes grey with fury. "The soldiers have found those we helped to escape."

Yes, Will thought. They have found them. And the slaughter would move north across the plain. Until the blood lust of the Seventh Cavalry was satisfied. Until the officers of the Seventh could control their men again. Or until every living thing that belonged to the village of Big Foot was dead.

As Siya-Ka was dead.

Will's mind was wild with grief. He stared at Red Bird. "Are we going to crouch here like rabbits and die when they find us? Or are we going to die like men? There are weapons on the dead down here in this draw."

He leaped down the hillside. As he did, the burning flood of tears he had held back so long scalded his eyes. He yelled as though he had gone mad. He screamed curses in English, taunts and insults in Sioux. Behind him came the half-score of braves, all that remained of the hundred and fifty who had lined up to be disarmed.

A hundred lodges down there, cut to ribbons, filled with holes by cannon and rifle fire. Two hundred dead and wounded scattered on the trampled ground.

A baby wailed continuously from its cradle on the back of its dead mother. An old man groaned somewhere.

Through the village went the men, unseen by those still pouring bullets and shot into it until they were clear of the village on the far side.

Will scarcely felt the kick of the rifle against his shoulder, but he saw a soldier rise, clutch his throat, then fall to the ground.

Around him his friends were falling, like toy warriors knocked down by a child. But Will went on, the empty rifle clubbed, and felt a head smash beneath its stock.

He saw a rifle in the hands of a mere boy soldier come to his shoulder. He saw the gaping muzzle and the wide, terror-stricken eyes behind it. He tried to leap aside, but it was too late.

The muzzle flash blinded him and the black smoke filled his lungs and made him choke. The impact of the bullet against his chest was like the kick of a horse, shocking, numbing, paralysing.

He felt his eyes rolling wildly, felt them focus again. Tears stood out in the eyes of the boy soldier and his soft mouth trembled like a woman's when she is about to weep.

He flung the rifle from him and watched Will

as though fascinated by his contorted face and staring eyes.

Suddenly Will could see him no longer. The sky reeled before his eyes, its black, hurrying clouds making but a brief impression on his mind.

He scarcely felt the impact of his body as it struck the ground. It was as though he had collapsed into a heap of feathers that cushioned his fall with their softness.

But he saw a man standing above him, rifle poised to smash his skull.

He felt no blows. Suddenly the sky was dark, as though night had fallen. His eyes were open, but they saw no light. And he was falling, into a bottomless pit of blackness.

He did not hear the soldier's words as the man turned away, "Hell, the son-of-a-bitch is already dead. That's good shootin', Frank."

Will seemed to be falling forever. His last thought was that when he stopped falling, he would be dead.

CHAPTER ELEVEN

Will didn't know how long he had lain this way. But when he could hear again, and feel again, the soldiers were past, moving through the village, and Will lay alone with the dead surrounding him.

His chest was on fire with pain and it was this, perhaps, that had brought him consciousness again. He turned his head, blinded temporarily by the pain resulting from even so small a move as this.

They had thought him dead, he realised. That was why his head had not been smashed by the soldier's rifle butt.

His vision returned, blurred and uncertain, and he saw their blue-clad backs disappearing among the tepees of the village.

The battle was done, the slaughter finished. All that now remained for Will was death.

He didn't mind even though he knew his dying would be slow and filled with pain. He would lie here all day to-day while the cold slowly froze his arms and legs. Always with him would be this pain, and as time passed, it would grow worse.

His head seemed to float apart from his body. He seemed to be dancing the Ghost Dance again, and again he saw a vision. The vision he wanted to see, he realised. A vision of Siya-Ka.

She came from the entrance to one of the tepees

and stood before it, looking around her at the terrible scenes of destruction and death. Then the shadowy form began to run. From body to body, and at each one she knelt.

And Will's ears could hear sound—that of a woman's terrible, agonising weeping.

A thought occurred to Will. He was alive, and through some miracle Siya-Ka was alive. Soon she would reach him and they could die together at least.

Consciousness slipped away and when it returned the vision—the form of Siya-Ka—was gone.

The sky faded. Again Will slipped into unconsciousness. When he regained it, he looked up into the blurred, almost formless face of a woman, a face streaked with blood and pain.

Tears clouded the woman's eyes and dripped into his face where they felt warm and soft, like summer rain. The blurring cleared.

He tried to rise, but pain and weakness held him motionless against the frozen ground. He heard a cry, "You live! You are not dead!"

For an instant she was silent. Then she cried, "I must get bandages I . . ."

He found the strength to grasp her arm. His voice was a croak. "No. They are gone but they will kill you. Lie here with me until you are sure they all are gone."

She removed his hand gently from her arm.

She cut away his shirt with her knife and peered at the wound. She sobbed once, a sound like an agonised intake of breath.

Will heard cloth tearing and a few moments later felt the sharpest, most excruciating pain he had ever known. He slipped into unconsciousness again.

When he came to, he was alone. All sound had gone from this place and it lay in dark and formless silence. He called back to his mind the memory of Siya-Ka, and clung to it as a drowning man clings to a floating branch.

Dawn came, and the sun climbed high. He floated between layers of consciousness and unconsciousness. The sun began to sink toward the rim of the world in the west. And as the sun ebbed, so did the tide of life ebb within Will's body.

He became weaker and his periods of lucidity were both shorter and more widely spaced. The sun set, and dusk crept across the land.

Sometimes he would hear a fitful wail, a moan of pain, or the dying rattle of breath in a wounded throat.

Death now seemed like a friend, to be welcomed when he came. Will was young and he had been strong. Weakness and helplessness were strange to him.

He heard the rattle of approaching wagons but he did not believe. Then at last, he saw the light of lanterns, and in them, the face of Siya-Ka, grey with fear and worry.

She saw his open eyes and immediately turned and began to scream. Another face appeared beside hers, one Will recognised as that of the Episcopal minister at Pine Ridge.

He knelt and laid blankets on the ground beside Will. He replaced Siya-Ka's bandaging with fresh bandaging of his own.

Will lost consciousness as they lifted him to the bed of a wagon. He remained unconscious during the all-night trip to Pine Ridge.

But Siya-Ka rode with him, warming his chilled body with her own, praying endlessly to Wakan Tanka to spare him.

He lay in a bed at Pine Ridge for five long days, fever-ridden and delirious. When his consciousness finally did return, he was so weak he couldn't lift his hand.

All this time, Siya-Ka stayed with him, refusing to leave even at the insistence of the minister and the Episcopal nuns.

Convalescence was slow and accompanied by pain. But Siya-Ka stayed with him. And the nuns read to him from the newspapers.

Americans all over the land had bitterly condemned the actions of the Seventh Cavalry that bloody day. They cried out for justice for the Sioux. By the time Will was able to sit up in bed, the Indian war was over.

General Nelson A. Miles took the credit, of course, claiming that his bottling up of the tribes within the badlands had starved them out. But from Siya-Ka, Will learned the truth. Standing Bear had ended the war by carrying the pipe of peace to the tribes in the badlands. At great risk he had done it, for if enough of the warriors there had refused to accept it, he would have been killed for his pains.

Afterward a steady stream of newspapermen and visitors came to the little Episcopal church at Pine Ridge where Will was and talked with him. They wrote his words down and published them in their papers. They shared his anger over the injustices done the Sioux and promised that something would be done.

The change began. But in Will occurred the greatest change. He accepted at last the truth—that the day of the prairie tribes was gone. He accepted the fact that he, like his father, must learn to live like the whites. When the day came at last when he could leave, the Reverend Cook offered him the use of a house belonging to the church and located not far from the Agency. He loaned him a wagon to take him and Siya-Ka to the house.

They were destitute, having nothing but the clothing the missionaries had given them, a quarter of beef also given them, and a few blankets which lay in the wagon bed.

But Will Jordanais did not feel poor. He looked at the sun, hot and bright in a sky as blue as the turquoise of the Navajo. He looked at the land, streaming and growing now under its warming rays. He looked at his wife, sitting so contentedly at his side.

She smiled and her hand came out to clasp his own. The warm-toned skin of her face grew pink and her eyes looked down. "I have news," she said. "Good Eagle will have a son."

Will's heart leaped and suddenly he laughed. "Good Eagle will have many sons," he said. "Many sons and many cattle and many friends, both among the Sioux and among the whites."

And suddenly he could not wait until they should come home, until Siya-Ka would once again run eagerly into his arms.

Center Point Large Print
600 Brooks Road / PO Box 1
Thorndike, ME 04986-0001 USA

(207) 568-3717

US & Canada:
1 800 929-9108
www.centerpointlargeprint.com